HER BILLIONAIRE CHEF

An Overnight Billionaire Bachelor Romance

By Laura Ann

This is a work of fiction. Similarities to real people, places, or events are entirely coincidental.

HER BILLIONAIRE CHEF

First edition. October 13, 2019.

Copyright © 2019 Laura Ann.

Written by Laura Ann.

DEDICATION

To the sister who's creative/crafting talent
makes me look like I'm all thumbs.
You're everything a big sister should be.
I love you.

ACKNOWLEDGEMENTS

No author works alone. Thank you Victorine,
You and your sister make it Christmas every time
I get a new cover. And thank you to my Beta Team.
Truly, your help with my stories is immeasurable.

PROLOGUE

“I can't decide if we're desperate idiots, or desperate geniuses,” Eli Truman grunted as he swung his sledgehammer into the stone wall.

“Does it really matter?” Nelson, his youngest brother, said with a laugh. “Either way, we're still here, covered in dust, dirt and who knows what else, renovating an ancient castle.” His eyes darted toward the shaking ceiling. “That's going to come down on us at any moment if you don't ease up with the wall toppling.”

Eli grunted again, but rested the sledgehammer at his feet.

“You two are the idiots. Everyone knows I'm the brains of this operation,” Hayden, the middle brother, said as he hefted an armful of lumber into the space they were working in.

Avangarde castle had become the brothers' last hope. Eli was fresh off a divorce, Hayden had recently gotten fired from his chef job in New York and Nelson had joined because he held no commitment elsewhere. Together, they had pooled their resources and purchased the crumbling structure of bricks they now stood in. The plan was to bring a section of it up to code and open a bed-and-breakfast.

Nelson rolled his eyes. “Knowing how to make whipped cream doesn't make you a genius.”

Hayden glared. “No, but knowing the difference between foie gras and paté might.”

“Give it a rest, guys,” Eli, ever the diplomat, said as he hefted the sledgehammer again. “After I get this wall down, we can see what we have to work with.”

With a loud grunt, he swung at the wall one last time. Dust rained from the ceiling and all three men ducked and covered their heads.

Once they had all stopped coughing, Nelson spoke. "Geez, Eli. Got anger much?"

Eli wiped sweat and dirt from his forehead. "Sorry. That stupid stone has been here for hundreds of years. It doesn't exactly want to come down."

Hayden cocked his head as he stared with narrowed eyes at the wall. "Dude, we might be in more trouble than we thought. It looks like you broke the wall."

"That was the whole point, *Genius*," Nelson sneered as he walked over to examine Eli's progress.

"Not that wall." Hayden dropped his lumber and made his way across the messy work site. "This one." He put his hand out and pushed against what appeared to be a depression in the stone. "Whoa." Hayden's eyes widened, and he stepped back, nearly tripping when the wall shifted inward showing a hidden opening.

"Dude! Seriously?" Nelson bounded across the room and stuck his head in the small door. "That's awesome!"

"What is it?" Eli asked as he carefully made his way over.

"Dunno," Nelson grinned over his shoulder. "But we should find out."

Hayden scowled. "Are you serious? There's probably rotting bodies or something in there." He folded his arms across his broad chest. "No, thank you."

Nelson rolled his eyes again. "Rotting bodies? No one has lived here for like a hundred years, any bodies would be complete dust by now, Genius."

"Stop calling me that," Hayden growled.

Nelson's eyebrows shot up. "You're the one who claimed you were so smart, just following your lead... Genius."

Hayden leaned in nose to nose with his little brother. "Don't make me get my carving knives."

Nelson gave a fake shiver. "Ooh, now I'm scared. A guy who spends his time in an apron and puffy hat is gonna hurt me."

Hayden reached out and grabbed Nelson, putting him in a headlock before he could react.

With a laugh and holler, Nelson grabbed Hayden's wrist and twisted his way out, using his years of martial art training to evade further attempts of imprisonment.

"CHILDREN!" Eli shouted, grabbing them both by the shoulders. "Knock if off for a minute, huh?" His face went back to the hidden door. "I think we should figure out what's going on here." He nodded his chin toward the hole. "If there are hidden rooms, they'll affect the structural integrity of the building and we need to know what we're dealing with."

"True enough," Hayden said, rolling his neck and swinging his arms as if he were warming up for a sports contest.

"Maybe you should stay here, Bro. We wouldn't want to have an accident and hurt your whisking arm or anything," Nelson said with a smirk,

Hayden glared and stepped forward, but Eli stopped him with a hand to his chest. "Where are the flashlights?"

Nelson hurried into the other room and was back in a few seconds. "Here we go! One for each of us. Sorry, Hay, I couldn't find your pretty princess one. It must still be packed in your luggage upstairs." He laughed. "Ouch!" He rubbed the back of his head where Eli slapped him.

"Knock it off, Squirt. One of these days I won't stop him from pounding you into the ground."

"Like a guy who went to school to wear a skirt could pound me," Nelson muttered while rubbing his head.

Eli turned his flashlight on and pushed the door open as far as it would go. The door was thick and after the first couple of inches, didn't move easily. The squeal of the hinges made it clear that the door hadn't been opened in many years.

With a deep breath, Eli stepped into the darkness. "Oh, man." He coughed a couple of times and swiped in front of his face. "Dang, the dust and cobwebs are thick."

"This is going to be epic," Nelson whispered. "How many dead people do you think we'll find?"

Hayden shook his head. "You're such an idiot."

"And you're such a girl!"

"Shut up," Eli growled. "Nelson, go grab that broom." He put his hand on his hip and flashed his light around. "Maybe I can use it to clear the cobwebs so we can actually walk in there."

"Coming right up, Boss." Nelson worked his way through the construction zone and grabbed a beat up broom sitting in the corner.

"Thanks," Eli murmured as he studied the secret passageway. He looked over his shoulder. "Here we go." Setting his jaw, he held the broom in front of him, swinging it slowly from side to side as he worked his way inside. "There's a staircase in here!" Eli called, surprise evident in his tone.

"Where does it go?" Nelson called back.

Hayden scowled. "How the heck is Eli supposed to know?" He shook his head. "Idiot," he mumbled.

"I meant for him to find out... why are you always so grumpy? You catch more flies with honey than vinegar dude. You, of all people, should know the difference between the two."

Hayden scowled and stepped into the space after Eli.

"Careful, these steps are pretty narrow," Eli's voice echoed slightly as it came up the stone walkway.

"Got it," Nelson yelled, leaning over Hayden's shoulder to answer.

Hayden flinched and covered the offended ear. Grumbling something under his breath, he stepped further into the darkness.

Slowly, the three brothers made their way down the dark and musty stairwell. The air felt heavy with moisture, and an aura of tension settled on each brother as they continued down the seemingly never-ending stairwell.

"This place is creepy." Nelson said as he glanced behind him at the darkness. "Oof!" Just as he turned back around he ran into something solid. "Dude! Why did you stop?" Nelson rubbed his chin where he had smacked into Hayden's head.

"Watch where you're going and you won't have that problem," Hayden muttered. "Eli stopped, so I stopped."

"There's a door," Eli called from the front.

All three brothers focused their flashlight beams to the front. A solid wood door, tall and straight, stood before them.

"Is it locked?" Hayden asked, his normally taciturn voice had lightened to awe.

Eli put his hand out and rested it on the dusty knob. Flexing his muscles, he twisted hard and the heavy door opened slightly. A puff of cold air hit the brothers in the face.

"Whoa..." Nelson breathed.

Eli glanced over his shoulder, his eyebrows furrowed together, before taking a deep breath and shouldering his way into the room.

"Eli? You still alive?" Nelson called out after a few moments of silence.

Hayden elbowed his baby brother in the chest. "Can you shut up for once?"

"What?" Nelson rubbed his chest. "It's a legitimate question."

Hayden looked at the ceiling and shook his head. "Come on," he growled. Slowly, they walked into the dark room.

Eli was standing only a few feet inside the doorway, still as a statue.

"What's going on?" Hayden slapped a hand on Eli's shoulder.

Eli's jaw was slack and his eyes focused into the darkness. Without saying a word, he pointed a finger in front of him. Nelson and Hayden followed his finger and focused their flashlights the same direction as their older brother.

Hayden's eyes widened and Nelson gasped.

"Dude, are you all seeing this?" Nelson's voice was quiet and shaky.

Both of his brothers nodded, but didn't speak.

"I don't think we're desperate anymore," Eli finally mumbled.

CHAPTER 1

Six Months Earlier

Hayden took the towel hanging from the tie at his waist and wiped his forehead with it. He rolled his neck and tried to get the kinks out of his shoulders. *Geez, that was a long night.*

The large, stainless steel kitchen was slowly closing down. Half of his workers had already gone home and the few that were left were doing their best to finish quickly. Tonight's dinner rush had lasted longer than usual and everyone was asleep on their feet.

Hayden fought a yawn and cracked his neck one more time for good measure.

"Good night, Chef," called the last of the young workers as they walked out the door.

Hayden nodded and followed them; double checking that the side door was locked. He walked through the kitchen, making sure everyone's work was up to snuff. Hayden had graduated from culinary school a couple of years prior and had made headlines when he was signed on as one of the youngest head chefs in New York City. People loved his food but the media quickly realized his personality wasn't as wonderful as his dishes. Hayden was a driven, focused individual, and he had no time to play nice for reporters.

Most days he wore a scowl, and those who lasted under his employ described him as someone who was obsessive about the details.

But I get results, he thought as he walked around the spotless area.

Finally satisfied that all was as it should be, he headed out to the dining area to turn off all the lights. *Ah, crud.* Hayden mentally rolled his eyes.

Joyce Keller, the owner of the restaurant Hayden worked at, sat at the bar, spinning a goblet of wine. The middle aged woman was very hands on with her restaurant, which diners loved and Hayden wouldn't have minded either, if she didn't feel that everything in the restaurant belonged to her... including him.

He spun on his heel to leave before she saw him, but it was too late.

"Just the man I've been waiting for," she purred. Joyce stood from her stool, not bothering to adjust the short black skirt that had ridden up when she sat. Her stilettos clicked on the marble floors as she strode his direction, her long, dyed blonde hair waving over her shoulders and back.

Hayden sighed and turned to face her, folding his arms and raising an eyebrow. His boss was a beautiful woman, but she was at least twenty years older than him and most of her looks had been put in surgically, to the point where Hayden couldn't tell what parts of her were real. *Not exactly what I'm looking for in a woman.* "What did you need, Mrs. Keller?"

She pushed her full, red lips out in a pout. Stopping right in front of him she dragged a manicured nail down his chest. "I think you know exactly what I need, Hayden." She glanced at him from under her fake eyelashes.

Hayden stepped back quickly. Her touch sent a jolt through him, and not the good kind. "And I know that I've made it clear that I'm not willing to cross that line." He turned around and headed back toward the kitchen.

"I made you who you are, you know," she called after him. She spoke in a low, cultured tone, but an underlayer of steel was easily heard.

Hayden paused mid-stride before turning back toward her with a frown. "Excuse me?"

Joyce smiled. "Your fame? Your notoriety? It's all thanks to me." Her smile fell and her eyes turned to ice. "And I can strip you of it quicker than I built you."

Hayden's dark eyebrows shot up. "*You* made me?" He growled. "I'm where I am because I'm the best. I push harder than anyone else and I don't stop until it's perfect. And you know it." He took a menacing step in her direction.

Joyce laughed. "Oh, Hayden. Don't think you can growl at me and I'll go running with my tail between my legs." She smirked. "Such naivety on a man isn't exactly attractive, Darling."

Hayden shook his head. "We're done here."

"Think carefully, Hayden. I can ruin you like that." She snapped her fingers. "Is your career really worth your morals?"

Hayden paused, his nostrils flaring. *Can she really hurt my career? Yes, she has connections, but I've climbed to the top through sheer grit and determination. Being fired won't kill me, will it?* His indecision must have shown on his face because Joyce straightened, jutting out her chest as a look of triumph crossed her face. Her look snapped Hayden out of his thoughts and pushed him over the edge.

"I think I'll take my chances," he said darkly before storming out of the room.

"Ahhh!" Joyce screamed and Hayden heard a crash, causing him to think she threw her wine glass.

"Good luck getting that stain out," Hayden muttered as he grabbed his coat and burst out the door to his car.

"HOLD ON, HAYDEN," ELI'S voice crackled across the line. "I can't understand you. Calm down and try again."

Hayden did his best to slow down his heaving chest, pulling air in through his nose and pushing it out through his mouth. His forehead was furrowed and his jaw clenched. He could feel his nostrils flare with every intake of breath. "Fine," he ground out. "Mrs. Keller fired me."

"What? Why the heck would she do that? You're the best new chef in New York!" Eli's incredulous tone made Hayden feel only slightly better.

"Be that as it may, she fired me." Hayden fell into his sofa and put an arm over his eyes.

"You still haven't told me why. Did you make her cry like you do your kitchen staff? Surely you know better than to do that to your boss, Hayden!" Eli's voice rose, and he was nearly shouting at the end of the sentence.

"Your trust in my level of intelligence is astounding, Eli," Hayden grumbled. "But no, I didn't make her cry." He paused. "At least not in the way you're implying."

"Then what *did* you do?"

Hayden cleared his throat. "I turned her down."

There was silence on the line.

"Are you still there?" Hayden asked.

"Yes. I'm just processing. You turned her down? Like what? She propositioned you?"

"You could say that," Hayden groaned.

"Either she did, or she didn't. Which is it?" Eli's tone had dropped and was almost an exact match for Hayden's.

"She's propositioned me dozens of times and finally got tired of me saying no. She gave me an ultimatum. My job or my principles."

"She can't do that. Maybe we should get a lawyer-"

"It's my word against hers," Hayden interrupted. "She's a well-known and respected business woman. I don't think we'd stand a chance."

Eli sighed. "Okay. So, just go work somewhere else. It sounds like that wasn't exactly an ideal work environment, anyway."

"I can't," Hayden said softly. The fight had drained him. His body felt heavy, like he had been dragged through the mud.

"You're at the top of your game. Of course you can get another job."

"No one will hire me. Joyce used her connections to completely blackball me. I've interviewed with half a dozen restaurants in the last couple of days and I keep getting the same message: Thanks, but no thanks."

"How do you know Joyce is behind it?"

Hayden sighed. "One of the guys I went to school with let it slip. No one in the culinary community will have me."

Eli sighed. "Why don't you sell your apartment and come out here to regroup for a bit. Melinda's been gone for a couple of months now, you might as well occupy the spare bedroom."

"Melinda's gone?" Hayden frowned as he thought of Eli's vicious wife. He'd never liked her, but it wasn't like he'd had much say in the matter.

"Yeah," Eli sighed. "Apparently, I'm a deadbeat who will never amount to anything. She took off with some hotel owner."

"Aww, Eli. I'm sorry." Hayden rubbed his face with his free hand.

"Yeah. It hasn't been good here for a while. It'll get better once the divorce paperwork goes through. Come on out and we'll figure out our next move."

"Right. Give me a few days. I'll shoot you a text with the details."

"Sounds good."

CHAPTER 2

Asmile played on Cadence's full, red lips as she pulled open one of the double glass doors at her father's business. The lobby was empty of people and her shoes echoed through the room. *Everyone must be out to lunch. Perfect.*

Walking over to the elevator, she punched the button and waited impatiently. She glanced around and admired the architecture of the space while the elevator took its time. The foyer was wide open with stunning hardwood floors that always gleamed as if they had just been polished. A large flower arrangement sat on the side of the receptionist's desk, its beautiful spring blossoms bringing color to the mostly white space. She straightened her pencil skirt and pushed her long, dark hair behind her ear.

DING.

Finally. Cadence stepped in and punched the sixth floor. Her father could probably be found in the penthouse on floor ten, but today, she wasn't here for him.

She glanced at the large rock on her left hand, admiring how the yellow lights of the elevator bounced off of its facets. Her smile dropped a little as she thought of the man who had put it there.

Ryan Woodward was tall, handsome, charismatic and wealthy. Every woman's dream. *Sort of,* Cadence thought. Ryan was her father's right-hand man and was not only poised to take over the law firm but also to follow in her father's political footsteps. *I might not love Ryan, but he'll be a good addition to the family. He's a nice guy, I'm sure we'll get along just fine. I mean, we've known each other since we were kids, surely we can make a good life together.* She pursed her lips. *Maybe after we eat,*

I can talk to him about my getting a job. I don't want to just be some trophy wife like my mother.

She straightened her shoulders and put her well-trained society smile back on her face. Her plan today was to surprise Ryan at work and take him to lunch. *The more time we spend as a couple the more chance we have of our relationship leading to something more.*

The elevator slowed to a stop and smoothly opened its doors, allowing Cadence to step into the hallway. She immediately turned right, heading straight for Ryan's office. A quick glance told her his secretary wasn't at her desk, so Cadence didn't bother to announce her presence.

She grasped the door handle and pushed it inward. "Ryan! I thought we could-" The words died on her lips.

"Cadence!" Ryan jerked away from the woman he had been kissing. He wiped his mouth and ran his hand through his hair. "I didn't know you were coming."

Cadence felt the blood drain from her head and she stiffened her knees to keep from slumping to the floor. "Apparently, not," she whispered.

"Excuse me," a feminine voice mumbled. Ryan's secretary darted around him and bee-lined for the door, racing past Cadence at lightning speed.

Cadence turned to watch her go.

"Hey, Babe," Ryan said in her ear as he wrapped his arms around her waist.

Cadence jumped back and nearly fell over in her heels. "Hey, Babe? Are you kidding me?"

Ryan frowned and stepped back.

"I just found you cheating on me with your secretary and you think I'm going to welcome your touch?" Cadence's normally sultry tones had risen higher than normal and the sounds echoed through the room.

"Hey!" Ryan patted the air with his hands. "Keep it down. It's not as bad as you think it is."

"Not as bad? Not as bad?" Cadence's light blue eyes widened. "I walk in to find you with a woman backed up against the wall and I'm supposed to believe it's not that bad?"

"Cadence..." Ryan's soothing tones grated on her nerves. "It's not like it meant anything. It's no big deal, Sweetie. It's all just part of the lifestyle."

Cadence jerked back like she had been slapped. "What do you mean just part of the lifestyle?"

Ryan put out his hands to either side. "Those at the bottom are always trying to get a piece of those at the top. It's just a bit of fun." He smiled and took a step toward her. "But it's you I'll come home to every night." He reached out and ran a finger along her jaw.

Cadence's stomach lurched and for a moment she thought she might throw up on Ryan's shoes. *It would serve him right, they probably cost a fortune.* "So, let me get this straight," she said through clenched teeth. "You think it's all right for you to play around during the day, as long as you come home to me at night?"

Ryan shrugged. "These little flings don't mean anything." He grabbed her around the waist and pulled her in. "It won't make any difference in our status as one of the most powerful couples in California."

Cadence stepped forcefully out of his arms. "Yes, well, I'm afraid that won't be happening." She didn't meet his eyes as she backed up and slipped the ring off her finger.

"What do you mean?" Ryan said through a forced laugh.

"I mean, I won't marry you. I won't stand idly by while you have affair after affair and then expect me to welcome you home in the evenings." Jerking her chin up, she met his panicked gaze head on.

"Now, Cadence-" He reached out for her.

"Goodbye, Ryan." She pressed the ring into his outstretched hand and spun on her heel. Without another word, she used her long, tanned legs to get her to the elevator as quickly as possible. As she walked by the secretary's desk, the woman had the good sense to duck her head down.

"He's all yours," Cadence said coldly.

Punching the button, Cadence waited for the elevator to reach her floor.

"Cadence, you can't leave like this. What will your father say?" Ryan's face was red and angry as he marched down the hall.

"He'd say good riddance to a cheating scumbag." With a scowl, she turned toward the emergency exit and pushed it open, using the stairs rather than waiting for the slow elevator. As she worked her way down the flights, she listened intently for footsteps that would indicate Ryan was following her, but she heard nothing.

Once she burst out of the building, she took in a much needed gulp of fresh, salty ocean air. Tears stung her eyes, but she bit her lip and refused to let them fall. *He's not worth it. It's not like you loved him.* She whimpered as she walked to the parking garage, rubbing her stinging heart. *Maybe not, but betrayal hurts no matter what.*

CADENCE SLOWLY ROSE from where she was sitting on her father's expensive leather sofa. "What do you mean I still have to marry him?" She was seething inside and her father appeared oblivious to her feelings.

Noah Everwood tilted his head, and a gave Cadence a look of pity. "Dear, you're overreacting."

"I caught him with his secretary!" Cadence threw her arms in the air. "How is that overreacting?"

He put his hands out. "So, he has some wild oats to sow. It won't last forever. Eventually he'll get too old to keep fooling around."

Cadence's jaw dropped. "I can't believe you're defending him. Cheating is wrong. Just plain wrong. How can you ask me to live with a man who doesn't respect me enough to stay true? I mean you've never-" Her eyes widened as a light bulb lit in her mind. "Are you telling me you've cheated on Mom?"

Noah had the good grace to blush as he cleared his throat and looked at the wall.

"Oh my word, you have! Unbelievable!"

"Now, Cadi-bear, bring your voice down."

"Don't you Cadi-bear me! Does Mom know?" Cadence folded her arms over her chest.

"Of course, she does," he stated calmly.

Her heart speed tripled. "She knows you cheat on her and yet she stays married to you? What kind of marriage is that?" Everything she thought she knew about her family vanished. She knew she had been raised in a bubble. Her father was beyond wealthy and Cadence had never wanted for anything. *Except attention and the chance to use my brain.*

She had been raised by nannies, who had filled in some of the gaps left from her parents lack of attention. She had gone to the best schools and had earned a Master's Degree in Finance, but even throughout all of it, she knew her parents planned for her to return home, marry Ryan, and become an elite, California Socialite. It wasn't Cadence's ideal life, but she thought her parents had only been looking out for her. *That's because I thought they were happy in this life, and they wanted me to be happy as well.* She frowned. *How could I have been so blind?*

"It's the type of marriage everyone has. Now, just calm down and let's talk this out rationally," her father insisted.

"No." Cadence threw back her shoulders and stuck her chin in the air.

Noah paused. "No?"

"You heard me. N-O. No. I won't marry that man. I won't marry into a sham of a marriage only to be left behind as he 'sows his wild oats.'"

She made quotation marks with her fingers to mimic her father's words. "I won't be a part of this."

Noah straightened to his full, intimidating height and folded his arms, scowling at his daughter. "Then just what do you expect to do? Ryan is going to take over my company and eventually run for office. Where do you think that will leave you when he does?"

She pushed up her chin. "I have an education. I'll get a job and take care of myself."

Noah laughed derisively. "You don't know the first thing about life, Cadence. You've been spoiled and pampered since you were born. Everything has been done for you. You have no way of taking care of yourself."

"I'll learn," she growled. Before her father could throw out any more insults that left Cadence in a puddle of tears, she stormed out of the room and went to her bedroom. Grabbing her luggage from her large, walk-in closet, she began throwing clothes inside.

She left the dozens of formals draping on their hangers and grabbed her business and casual clothes. "Pretty sure I won't need a fifty-thousand dollar dress for a normal company party," she muttered as she worked.

Once she was packed, she glanced around at her room, memorizing the look and feel of the space she had lived in for so long. Memories tugged at her mind and she found herself blinking back tears.

"Just where do you think you're going?" Her mother's low voice broke Cadence's reverie.

Cadence turned, grabbed the handles of two of her suitcases and pushed past her mother into the hall. "Away," she stated.

"What do you mean, away? Cadence? Cadence!" Arianna Everwood chased her daughter down the hallway. "Stop this instant and tell me what is going on, you ungrateful child."

Cadence paused, then slowly turned to look at her. "Did you know Dad has cheated on you?"

Arianna stiffened and began to fiddle with the rings on her fingers. "We'll, it's not as if anyone's perfect," she defended.

Cadence's stomach dropped, and she shook her head. "Why do you stay with him? Why do you hang around if you know he's not faithful?" A tear trickled down her cheek. "You've done the same thing, haven't you? You've had your own affairs."

Arianna's arms dropped and her chin went up. "I have a good life here. I know what it's like to have nothing."

Cadence held her breath. Her mother never spoke about her childhood. Cadence had never met her parents or grandparents. She knew her family came from Mexico and that they had been farm workers. But once Arianna caught the attention of the young and handsome Noah Everwood, she had turned her back on her poverty stricken family and never looked back.

"If I left your father, I'd be right back where I started," she hissed. "There's no way I'm going to sacrifice all of this just because of a few indiscretions, no matter who made them."

Cadence's chin slumped to her chest. "Money. It's all about the money and power, isn't it?"

Arianna huffed and threw her hands up. "What else is there?"

Cadence just stared at the woman who had given birth to her. The woman who had passed on her low, sultry voice and exotic looks that drew attention wherever Cadence went. The only visible thing Cadence had inherited from her father was her height.

Her mother's petite frame screamed of elegance and feminism. Something Cadence had always been a little envious of. Even as a middle-aged woman, Arianna Everwood turned heads, and she loved every minute of it. But right now, Cadence felt sorry for her. *How can she live like this? How can she stand there and tell me that diamonds and a big house are worth more than love and loyalty? The exact emotions I've been searching for my whole life.*

"Goodbye, Mother." Turning back toward the hall, Cadence dragged her suitcases down the stairs to the garage while her mother screeched in the background. As Cadence rolled through the kitchen, she called out to one of the staff. "George, could you please go grab the rest of my luggage and bring it to my car?"

"Yes, Ma'am," he murmured, then quickly followed her directions.

Once Cadence was loaded up, she thanked the gentle butler and hopped in her car. Before anyone could stop her, she tore out of the garage and down the driveway. Once she was out of the estate by a few miles, she pulled over to the side of the road and let the tears that had been pooling for the last hour loose.

For several minutes, Cadence sobbed into her hands, lamenting everything she had learned and everything she had left behind. Her tidy little world might not have been ideal, but it was hers. It was comfortable and familiar. Now everything had been turned upside down and Cadence's sense of direction was lost. The people she trusted had turned out to be complete strangers. *How did all this happen? How did I never see it?*

Once the tears finally slowed down, she took in a calming breath and grabbed a tissue from her dashboard. Pulling down the visor, she cringed when she saw herself in the mirror. Quickly, she cleaned her face then stared.

"All right, Cadence. You are a strong, capable woman. You don't need your father's money. You don't need your mother's support. And you definitely don't need Ryan's affection. You can make it on your own. And you will." She glared at herself in the mirror. "You. Will."

Pushing aside her broken heart, and the fear of the unknown, she nodded, flipped up the visor, put the car in gear and pulled back out onto the road.

"And you will never trust another rich man again."

CHAPTER 3

"I must say, Ms. Everwood, your resume is quite interesting. Your education is impressive, but you have held no previous jobs and thus have no references other than professors you studied under a couple years ago." Eli raised an eyebrow and glanced at Cadence over the papers in his hands.

Cadence tried to ignore the way her shirt was getting damp under her arms and the trickle of sweat she felt running between her shoulder blades. She gripped her fingers together in her lap to keep them from trembling as she sat straight up in her seat. "I understand, Mr. Truman. Truth is, I got an education because it was expected of me. My parents never planned for me to work and so I have no experience. But I think you will find that if you speak to my professors, I am a quick learner and a studious person. I understand it would be a risk to offer me my first job, but I promise you I can handle it. I'm professional and driven and I'm excellent with numbers." She hoped her voice came off as confident and not arrogant. She knew that offering her father's name would go a long way toward getting her a job, but she had an overwhelming desire to do this on her own. *I am going to earn this. I refuse to use my family name or connections to build my life from.*

Eli hummed and went back to looking at the papers. After a few moments of silence, he put them down, rubbed the bridge of his nose and sighed. "I'm going to be frank with you, Ms. Everwood." His piercing grey eyes bore into hers. "My brothers and I are drowning a bit. You probably heard the story of how we came into our wealth?"

Cadence nodded. The whole world had heard the fantastic story of how the Truman brothers had accidentally discovered a room full of hidden treasure when they were renovating the Avangarde Castle.

The media had dubbed them "The Overnight Billionaire Bachelors". All three men were handsome and single and the woman population had been going nuts ever since.

"Then you'll understand that although each of us has our different strengths, none of us are any good with numbers. We are in desperate need of someone to keep track of our business." He sighed and sunk back in his leather chair. "Maybe it's because we were raised middle class or because having access to so much money is still new, but I have this fear that if we're not careful, we will run ourselves into the ground, despite the amount of zeros in our bank account." He squished his lips to one side. "You must wonder why I'm telling you this."

Cadence nodded again, working to keep the hope inside of her from showing on her face.

"Truth is, you're the first woman who has come in and hasn't tried to hit on me."

Cadence's jaw dropped. *I mean, Mr. Truman is handsome enough, but he's rich, which means he's automatically off my list. Not to mention I feel no draw to him at all.* "I'm sorry, Sir. That must be horrible."

Eli chuckled ruefully. "You have no idea. Anyway," he brushed the topic aside, "my point is. We need someone and I think you might be it. I understand you have no real world experience, but your grades were excellent, the program you went to is one of the top in the country and, truth be told, you look like you could use a break."

Cadence stiffened. "Excuse me?"

Eli shrugged. "I meant no disrespect, but it's easy to see you're fighting something." His eyes darted down to the paper and back up to her. "You have provided the absolute minimum amount of personal information you can and you have offered no friends or even acquaintances as references."

Cadence stared Eli directly in the eyes. "Sometimes, a person has to make their own way in the world."

Eli nodded understandingly. "And that is why I think you can do the job." He stood and offered his hand. "Welcome to the team, Ms. Everwood. I look forward to working with you."

Cadence allowed a small smile to cross her lips, but she held the shouts of joy and elation inside. "Thank you, Sir." She shook his hand. "I won't disappoint you."

Eli nodded and led her over to the door. "Can you start Monday?"

"Absolutely."

"Is your commute going to be doable? I realize we aren't close to much of anything."

Cadence hid the panic she felt at his question. Truth was she had been alternating between sleeping in her car and staying in cheap hotels as she scoured the area for jobs. It had been sheer luck that a newspaper had been left at the table she occupied at a cafe the other day. The jobs listings had led her here, but technically, she didn't have a place to stay. "I, uh," she cleared her throat. "I'm still looking for a place, I'm new to the area."

Eli paused before he opened the door and pursed his lips. "We have a couple of old cottages on the property that aren't in use." He kept his hand on the doorknob but turned to look at Cadence. "They aren't fancy. They were built thirty-plus years ago and were mostly used as hunting lodges. I'd be happy to have one cleaned up and let you stay there."

Cadence's heart leapt. The idea of having her own space, no matter how small or dumpy it was, was so foreign and yet so exciting, she wasn't sure how to wrap her head around it. "What would you be asking for rent?"

Eli shook his head. "How about we just consider it a perk of the job? After all, we are a resort. I don't think it's that unusual for workers to live on resorts."

Cadence fought the desire to bite her lip. *Keep cool.* "That seems very generous. I'm not really sure what to say."

Eli shrugged. "It no big deal. There are about three cabins scattered around the property that we aren't sure what to do with. I had already thought about offering one to our landscaper since he's taking on a full time position. You'd actually be doing us a favor, this way they will stay in better repair, not to mention visitors to the resort won't go poking their noses around."

After his explanation Cadence felt lighter and more confident in taking him up on the offer. *If he's offering the same perk to other workers, then it's no big deal for me to say yes.* "Thank you," she said. "I accept."

Eli grinned and shook her hand. "After you see it, you might not be so grateful. It's a little rough around the edges, but we'll take care of that soon. I'll send a cleaning crew immediately, and you can move in tomorrow if you want. If need be, we'll look at doing other repairs as soon as is necessary."

"I'm sure it will be great."

Eli nodded and opened the door.

"What have we here?" A deep voice asked from the hallway.

Cadence's pulse skyrocketed at the honeyed tones of the voice and she had no control over her eyes as they shot toward the source. *Holy cow.* A tall, dark headed man stood with his arms folded, studying her intently. His eyes were as dark as his hair and they seemed to penetrate her straight to the core. As she studied his thick, black brows, straight nose and strong jawline, her eyes reluctantly shot back to Eli. *This has to be one of his brothers.*

"Hayden!" Eli said cheerfully, despite his brother's grimace. "Meet, Ms. Everwood. She's been interviewing for the finance position."

Clenching her jaw and putting on her business face, Cadence stuck out her hand. "Nice to meet you, Mr. Truman."

Hayden stared at her hand then back up at her. Although you could tell he and Eli were brothers, Hayden was broader through the shoulders and the way he folded his arms emphasized the size of his biceps.

Slowly, as if he were worried she would bite, he took her hand and gave it a hard shake before releasing it quickly.

Tingles from his touch ran up her fingers and Cadence fought the desire to shake her hand. *Don't even think about it, Cadence. He's wealthy and handsome. Everything you've sworn off.*

Hayden raised an eyebrow. "You don't look old enough to handle a job this size."

Oh. I see how it is.

"Hayden," Eli groaned and pinched the bridge of his nose.

Cadence straightened her spine and took a step toward the intimidating man. "Age has nothing to do with ability. If I recall correctly, you were awfully young to be appointed a head chef. Surely you don't think you are the only one who can handle a tough job straight out of school, do you?" Immediately, she bit her tongue. *You're going to lose the job before you've even started, you idiot! Why in this world would you say something like that?*

To her surprise, Eli chuckled. "Well, it looks like we're all going to get along just fine. Ms. Everwood, I'll be in touch." He waved her down the hall toward the entrance of the resort.

"Thank you, Mr. Truman." Without glancing at Hayden again, she took off and headed straight for her car. It wasn't until she had gotten out onto the main road that she let herself blow out the breath she had been holding.

"Good grief, Cadence. That was ridiculous. You've only been on your own for a few weeks, but all it took was a look from one handsome man and you nearly melted. Get a grip, girl," she growled. With a shake of her head, she headed to the nearest town, allowing herself to feel excited about only having to sleep in a hotel one more night.

HAYDEN WATCHED THE gorgeous woman walk down the hall and disappear around the corner of the large foyer. *Dang, she's got a*

tongue that matches her looks. When he looked back at Eli, he found his brother smirking with his arms folded.

"What?" Hayden scowled.

"Nothing," Eli said innocently.

Hayden rolled his eyes. "Sure." He glanced at his watch. "Wish me luck, I've got another round of kitchen interviews in the next few minutes."

Eli groaned and rubbed his forehead. "These stupid meetings are killing me. Half of them are women looking for a date instead of a job."

Hayden nodded. "Yeah. I'm having the same trouble."

"Good luck. I'm glad I have a break for the next hour." Eli slugged Hayden in the shoulder then stepped back into his office and shut the door.

With a deep breath, Hayden headed back toward the restaurant built into the resort. When they had renovated the castle, they had taken the largest ballroom and turned it into a dining area. Old world charm met sleek modernism in the open room. High stone walls connected to polished marble floors. A massive chandelier hung from the ceiling while individual candles sat at each table. The artwork that adorned the walls were mostly landscapes, with mountains, trees and rivers, reminiscent of the view just outside the castle.

After Hayden sat himself at the booth he had commandeered for his interviews, he looked through the stack of applications. His mind wandered as he glanced at dozens of similar answers.

Ms. Everwood's tall, willowy frame sat in his mind's eyes. Her dark hair was pulled back into a business-like bun, but it was easy to see that it was thick and silky. Her blue eyes stood out in stark contrast to her dark lashes and light brown skin. The make-up she wore only enhanced their color. Her lips were shaped like a rosebud and the red lipstick she wore accentuated their plumpness.

Hayden whistled low under his breath. *Shoot, she's a stunner. Too bad it looked as if her face would crack if she smiled.* He shook his head. "Just what I don't need."

CHAPTER 4

Cadence put the last of her clothes in the small dresser in her new cabin. With a smile and a sigh of contentment, she surveyed her surroundings. "Mine. This is mine and no one else's."

The cabin was tiny with one bedroom, a matchbox kitchen and just enough room for a small sofa in front of the television. After the cleaning crew had gone through, Cadence had had a chance to inspect the cabin and she asked Eli not to change anything.

The kitchen appliances were dated, but still worked. The sofa had been covered in a plastic slipcover, so it was in good shape. Eli had insisted that he buy a new mattress and Cadence hadn't fought him on that, but it had quickly been delivered, along with new bed linens and Cadence was settling herself in.

She had had to pare down her clothes since they wouldn't fit in the tiny closet, but her new found sense of freedom wouldn't allow that minor setback to keep her from feeling good about her move.

Her phone buzzed, interrupting Cadence's thoughts, and she walked to the bed to glance at the screen.

She growled when she saw Ryan's name and picture come through.

"He's got a lot of nerve," she mumbled, declining the call. She sighed and walked into the sitting area to plop down on the couch. She had spoken to her parents just yesterday. Just long enough to let them know she was safe and had found a job. When her mother had began to shout about her hurting the family name, she had ended the call and refused to pick up when she had called back. "My parents have a right to know that I'm okay, but that dirty, rotten scumbag doesn't," she muttered.

Ryan had only called twice during her first week on the road, so she was surprised he was trying again after all this time. *It's no skin off my nose. I'm free of handsome, rich men who think they can do anything they want.*

Grabbing an apple out of the bowl on her counter, Cadence munched while she looked over the files Eli had sent her. Her head swam as she looked at the numbers, and she did her best to stay calm.

"You can do this. It might take a little while to get on top of things, but you'll be fine." Determination ran through her after her little pep talk. Sticking in her headphones, she turned on her favorite instrumental music and started sorting through the data.

CHAPTER 5

One Year Later

CADENCE SAT IN THE comfortable leather chair in her office and narrowed her eyes as she studied the spreadsheet in front of her. Her job had been overwhelming when she had first started, but after a few internet searches and refresher courses on her college classes, she had settled in quite nicely.

She snorted. *Unless you count my relationship, or lack thereof, with Hayden.* Life had become fairly routine unless she passed the handsome man in the hallway or had to speak to him about the budget for the restaurant. Every time they met, sparks flew. *And not the good kind.* "Now, if I could just stop drooling over him," she mumbled as she worked.

Despite the fact that lightning flashed every time they were in the same room, the past year had not been long enough for Cadence to get rid of her initial attraction to him. Her heart rate still picked up when he was near, her skin grew flushed and her breathing became shallow. Not to mention, he seemed to work extra hard to get a reaction out of her. Cadence was normally a fairly calm individual, but between Hayden's constant provoking and her own anger at thinking him attractive, she always seemed to lose her temper when he was near. *So ridiculous. I should have outgrown this kind of thing ages ago.*

Cadence shoved Hayden out of her thoughts and went back to her work. After a few minutes she froze. "What in this world?" She double checked the numbers again and frowned. "What has he been buying?"

The spending numbers for the restaurant were almost double their normal amount. "Why would it jump up so much in such a short amount of time?"

Needing answers, Cadence shut off her computer and headed out of her office. It took no time at all for her to arrive at Eli's door and knock.

"Come in," Eli's smooth voice answered.

"Hey, Eli." Cadence opened the door and leaned her head inside his office. "I have a quick question."

Eli leaned back in his seat. "Alright, shoot."

"The restaurant numbers are extra high this month. Do you know if Hayden has done something different that I wasn't aware of?"

Eli sighed and ran a hand through his hair. His new gold band flashed in the light and Cadence felt a small flash of jealousy. *Stop it, Cadence.*

"I told Hayden he should let you know what he was doing. Apparently, he didn't follow my advice." Eli gave a regretful grin. "Hayden found some rare truffles or something that he wanted to purchase. He told me they would cost a small fortune and warned me the bill would be high."

Cadence's eyebrows shot up. "He bought what?"

"Truffles? Mushrooms? Something like that."

Cadence felt her frustration at the obstinate brother start to simmer. "Thanks," she said curtly, then quickly turned and started back down the hall. "Of all the-" She couldn't even finish her sentence. "Mushrooms! He spent thousands of dollars on mushrooms?" She shook her head and veered toward the kitchen. "Someone is going to have to reign in his crazy ideas. It might as well be me."

"YOU CALL THAT DICED?" Hayden Truman's eyes were narrowed and his brows scrunched. The edge of his mouth was pulled up into a sneer as he inspected the work of one of his new kitchen helpers.

The young man blinked rapidly. Glancing down at the carrots, his wide eyes jerked back up to Hayden. "Uh, yeah. I mean, yes. Yes, Chef."

Hayden could smell the worker's fear. The salty scent of sweat mingled with the tantalizing aroma of fresh soup and rising bread in the noisy kitchen. With a growl, Hayden moved in for the kill. "Massacre is more like it. Your knife is dull, your pieces aren't uniform, you-"

"Leave the boy alone," a low feminine voice sighed. "Being a millimeter off from each other isn't going to make them taste any different."

Hayden closed his eyes and pulled in a long breath through his nose. *Her.* He stood slowly from where he had been looming over the cowering worker. Straightening the lapels of his white, chef's coat, Hayden turned to look at the only woman who had ever managed to turn his head.

Cadence Everwood stood a couple feet from him, appearing like a goddess even in her business attire. There was nothing unprofessional about her clothes, but even the conservative pencil skirt and sleek bun in her hair couldn't detract from her jaw-dropping looks. Hayden's temperature spiked just looking at her, but he would die before admitting it out loud.

"If you're done making people cry for the day, we need to talk." Her voice held a hint of challenge that never failed to bring out Hayden's competitive streak.

Rising to her bait, he kept his eyes pinned on her, but jerked his head at the assistant. "You can go."

With a slight whimper, the young man darted away from what was bound to be an explosive situation.

"Happy now?" Hayden asked with a smirk, knowing it would tick her off.

"One less person to replace later this week," Cadence sniffed. Turning toward the doorway, she raised a brow. "Coming?"

Hayden walked into her personal bubble, stopping nearly nose to nose. "After you," he dropped his voice to an intimate level.

Pinching her lips, Cadence spun on her heel and clipped out of the kitchen, down the hall and into her office.

Hayden snickered, knowing his boorish manners drove her crazy, but there was something so enticing about her flushed cheeks and the fire that snapped in her eyes when he riled her up.

"To what do I owe the pleasure of this invitation?" He asked in a snarky tone as he walked in and plopped himself on one of the chairs sitting opposite her desk.

Cadence took a paper that was sitting in front of her, spun it around and pushed it toward him.

Hayden leaned forward and glanced at the numbers. "Should I understand what all this means? I thought you were the accountant."

That blush Hayden enjoyed crept up her cheeks. "Obviously, I mistook your level of intelligence," Cadence snapped. "This chart shows the charges from the restaurant for the last few months. If you'd bothered to read it, you would see there is a massive uptick in what you have been spending."

Hayden sat back and folded his arms over his chest. "I fail to see the problem."

"Seriously? You guys hired me to keep an eye on the money in this resort. Well, I'm watching it fly right out the window as you go nuts buying all those stupid mushrooms you found across seas."

Hayden's amusement at their banter died an instant death. The temper he was known for began to boil and he had to clench his teeth to keep from ripping into the woman across from him. "Those mushrooms, as you call them, are actually rare, exotic truffles. Do you have any idea how hard it was to find those? Let alone acquire them?"

Cadence threw the computer glasses she was wearing down on the desk. "Do you have any idea how much money you have spent doing so? You've spent tens of thousands of dollars over the last few weeks, Hayden! Either those 'truffles,'" Cadence made quotation marks with her fingers, "are made of gold, or you had better have bought enough for the next ten years."

Hayden rolled his eyes. "Like they would keep that long. I bought a couple of pounds worth."

Cadence gasped, her jaw hanging open like a gaping fish. "A couple of- this is a joke. This has to be a joke." She narrowed her eyes. "I don't find it funny. What did you actually spend the money on? The IRS is going to kill us if you've been putting personal expenses under the restaurant."

"Your opinion of me warms my heart," Hayden sneered. "I hate to break it to you, but the only expenses under the restaurant account are restaurant expenses. Those truffles are hard to find and even harder to buy." Hayden stood and leaned forward over the desk. "Do you have any idea how many people wanted those delicacies?"

Cadence stood slowly, meeting him eye for eye. "Then perhaps you should have let them have the nasty things. They look like dirt and smell even worse! Anyone who is willing to pay thousands of dollars per pound for something so disgusting should have their head examined."

"Of all the uncultured-"

"Hayden!" Eli's commanding tone broke through Hayden's angry haze.

Both Cadence and Hayden snapped straight and jerked their heads toward the doorway.

"I happen to know mother taught you better than that," Eli stated, daring his brother to disagree.

Hayden clenched his fists, but nodded. *I can't think straight around her. She messes with my head.*

"Ms. Everwood, while I appreciate your efforts to keep the numbers on track, Hayden has assured me that using those 'nasty things' in his dishes will not only elevate the food but allow him to charge enough to recoup the outrageous amount spent on something a pig dug out of the ground."

Hayden snorted at Eli's description, but folded his arms and shot a smug look at Cadence.

"However, myself and the entire resort heard enough of your fight to know that neither he nor I bothered to tell you those same words, so your frustration is understandable."

"Thank you, Eli. I appreciate your explanation and I apologize for my behavior. It was unprofessional and uncalled for. It won't happen again." Cadence kept her face down, and she smoothed a non-existent wrinkle in her skirt. Her voice sounded truly contrite as she spoke.

Hayden's eyes narrowed. *Oh, now she acts all meek and agreeable. One word from Eli and she agrees with everything.* A hot stream of jealousy poured through Hayden, the strength of it shocking him. With a growl, he stuffed it to the back of his mind and stormed toward the door.

He shoved past his brother and turned to head back toward the kitchen.

"Hayden, wait up," Eli called as he closed Cadence's door.

"What?" Hayden said gruffly.

Eli grinned as he put a heavy hand on Hayden's shoulder. "You're not going to win her if you keep snapping at her."

Hayden jerked out of Eli's reach as if he had been seared like a tuna filet. "What the heck are you talking about? I'm not looking to win anybody! Especially not some stuck-up numbers secretary who can't keep her nose out of my business."

Eli scowled. "That woman in there has one of the best heads for numbers I have ever seen and you would do well to stay on her good side. Under her care, the resort is more profitable than we could have predicted and I have no intention of losing her. If you don't want to man up to your feelings, fine, but try to keep down the fighting, huh? Find a different way to get rid of your attraction to her."

"You think I'm attracted to her?" Hayden scoffed. "No thanks, she's not my type."

"Well that's a relief, because the feeling is absolutely mutual," Cadence retorted from her doorway.

Eli's head hung in shame at Cadence hearing their conversation, but Hayden refused to cower. Folding his arms across his chest, he stared the stunning woman down.

Cadence mimicked his stance. "You should know that despite how thick these walls are, the doors are not quite as good at blocking sound. If you don't want me to hear what you are saying, I would suggest standing somewhere other than in front of my office to do it."

Hayden smirked. "So, noted."

Cadence's lips pinched and her chest heaved at his smug attitude. "And you can rest assured, Hayden, that I wouldn't date you if you were the last man on Earth."

Hayden sauntered over to her and grinned. "You know, I've always enjoyed a good challenge."

Panic ran through Cadence's eyes before she schooled them into cool disdain. "Who said anything about a challenge?"

"I believe you did, when you said you wouldn't date me if I was the last man on Earth."

Cadence's nostrils flared. "It was a statement."

Hayden shrugged and tilted his head with a carefreeness he didn't feel. Being this close to her was causing his pulse to speed up and an overwhelming urge ran through him to reach out and touch her soft skin. When he took a breath, he could smell her citrusy perfume. *It's perfect. Sweet with a tangy side.* "We'll see."

Cadence's hands clenched into tight fists and a dark pink spread across her cheeks.

Feeling empowered, Hayden gave her a wink and swaggered back toward the kitchens.

"I'm surrounded by toddlers," Eli groaned as Hayden walked away.

The sentiment made Hayden grin, but he bit back the laugh that wanted to follow. Cadence Everwood had been stealing Hayden's concentration ever since she arrived at the resort a year ago. Not only was she beautiful, but her penchant for fighting him on everything only caused him to be more attracted to her. Half the time, he picked fights just to see fire flash through her eyes. *She should have known better than to bring out my competitive side. Not only do I not back down from a challenge, I never lose. Someone has to knock Ms. Numbers off her high horse, and apparently, I'm just the guy to do it. And if that means spending more time irritating the lovely Ms. Everwood, then I suppose I'll just have to make that sacrifice.*

CHAPTER 6

Cadence couldn't seem to get Hayden's comments about 'accepting her challenge' out of her mind. The strong, independent part of her brain was furious. "I left home to get away from men exactly like him," she grumbled. "I don't need a man to complete me. I can do this on my own." *No matter how good looking he is.*

Despite her constant pep talks, there was a small part of her brain that argued. *Yeah, you can do it on your own, but how does that make you feel when you sit in front of your tiny television, eating ice cream all by yourself night after night?*

Cadence pushed away from her desk, frustrated with her lack of concentration. Grabbing her tiny rake, she began drawing patterns in the small sandbox she kept on her desk. "Mmm... I miss the beach. Washington beaches just aren't the same. They're so cold, not at all like the warm California beaches." She pursed her lips. "Maybe I should take a day off and go spend some time in the sand." *Just another way to be lonely.* That voice whispered at her.

"Ugh!" She dropped the rake and plopped her head on the desk. "All right. So I'm lonely. I haven't been on a date for over a year. I haven't seen my family in the same amount of time. I have almost no friends and the only guy I'm attracted to is a stuck up jerk who thinks I'm a challenge." She snorted. "My mother would be appalled. What am I saying? She *is* appalled. She's appalled I have a job instead of hanging off Ryan as his arm candy. Dad's appalled I won't take Ryan back. And I'm appalled I dropped one entitled rich boy only to find myself drooling over another."

Her phone buzzed, and she jerked her head up. When she saw the number she groaned. "Speak of the devil." She pushed the reject button. "No. No. And no!"

Ryan had taken to calling once a week despite the fact that she never picked up. He never left a message, never sent a text. *If he wanted to speak to me so badly, he'd figure out another way.*

Her phone went off again. "You've got to be kidding me!" Cadence picked it up, ready to answer and tell him to leave her alone, when she realized it wasn't Ryan. *Not that it's much better.*

"Hey, Dad," she tried to put some pep into her tone. Despite her frustrations with her life, Cadence had no desire for her father or mother to know what was going on. If they sensed any disappointment with her new found freedom, the pressure to come home would quadruple.

"How's my baby girl?" Her father's voice boomed over the line.

Cadence winced and pulled the phone away from her ear a little. "Just fine, thanks. How are you and mom?"

"Well... well. We miss you though. Your mother has been asking when you're going to come home."

When you stop asking when I'm getting together with Ryan. "Maybe I can come home and visit during one of our down times, but right now we're pretty busy."

Noah Everwood sighed. "Visit. I'm not sure that's what she had in mind."

Cadence gave into the urge to roll her eyes. "That's what grown children do, Dad. They visit their parents. I have a life here and I'm not ready to give that up."

"So you've said. But I don't mind telling you you've made a mistake, Hon."

Cadence shook her head. *He's never going to let it go!*

"Look, Cadi-bear. We love you. We only want what's best for you."

"What's best for me is to have my own life, which I do. Most parents would be proud that their child was using the expensive education they had provided," she spoke through clenched teeth.

"That education was to give you credibility in the public eye. It wasn't meant to be used to stay away from home."

Cadence huffed. "I'm afraid we're going to have to agree to disagree. Thanks for checking in on me. I'll talk to you later." She quickly hung up before he could stop her.

Dropping the phone on her desk, she grabbed her rake again. "Sun... sand... peace..." Slowly, the tension began to ebb as she repeated those words over and over, but the ache in her heart didn't move.

"Why can't they want what I want? Just because I don't want their lifestyle, I'm the bad guy?" She felt the prick of tears at the never-ending argument. "How can he say he loves me in one breath and then turn around and say I should come home the next?" She let out a shaky breath. "I won't do it. Living the lie they live would be even lonelier than I am now."

When her phone buzzed yet again, Cadence groaned loudly. "Just give up already!" She pushed the accept button while in the middle of yelling.

"Um, I'm sorry. What am I giving up?" Oliver Stevenson's slightly nasal voice asked over the line.

Embarrassment flooded Cadence, hot and swift. *Oh man. Can this day get any worse?* "Hey... sorry Oliver. I thought you were someone else." She cleared her throat. "What can I do for you?"

Oliver was a fellow accountant she had met through an online course she had taken when she first started the job at Avangarde. Although he worked mainly with retirement accounts, his help had been invaluable as she had been refreshing her studies and they had kept in touch from time to time, using each other for ideas or fact checking.

"Well, after your outburst, I'm not sure now is the best time to ask you."

Cadence closed her eyes. She could feel her cheeks flaming and was grateful they were on the phone rather than in person where he would be able to see her reaction. "No, now's fine. I'm really sorry. Go ahead and say what you need to."

"Okay, well…" He sneezed.

"Bless you," Cadence murmured.

"Thank you. Allergies."

She heard a snuffling noise before he came back on the line.

"I was wondering if you would like to have dinner with me this Friday?"

Cadence paused. *Uh…* Her mind spun. Even though they met online, they had discovered Oliver only lived thirty minutes away from the resort, so they had met in person a couple of times already, but it had all been business related.

"Are you still there?"

Cadence snapped to attention. "Yeah. Sorry. Um, dinner. Dinner would be good. Thank you for asking. When did you want to go?"

"I said this Friday."

Cadence slapped her palm to her forehead. *Get it together, dummy!* "Oh, sorry. I guess I'm a little distracted today. Friday is great. When and where?"

"I'll let you pick. Why don't you think about it and shoot me a text?"

Thank heavens he's not the type of guy who's easily offended. "Sounds great. I'll get back to you soon."

"Thanks." He hung up.

Cadence closed her eyes and rubbed her temples. "How do I get myself into these situations?"

"Pretty sure it doesn't take much effort," Hayden's smooth voice sounded from her doorway.

"What? Hayden! Couldn't you have knocked?" Cadence scowled at the intrusion. *How long has he been listening in?*

Hayden raised an eyebrow and stared at her while he reached out and knocked on the door. "Better?"

Cadence's eyelids fluttered as she fought the temptation to roll her eyes. "What do you need?"

"Now that is quite the question." He gave a crooked smile and Cadence's heart skipped a beat.

Stop it! She scolded herself. *He's so far off limits, it's not even funny.*

When Cadence didn't rise to his bait, he got down to business. "In order to avoid another blow up, I thought I would come tell you that I'm purchasing a new set of knives, so you can expect to see that on the inventory this month." He smiled widely. "Happy now?"

Cadence blinked and fought not to sigh at how handsome he was when he smiled. "Okay. Although I fail to see how that's going to change your spending much." She shrugged. "Knives only cost what, a couple hundred for a good set?"

Hayden's eyebrows shot up and he barked out a laugh. "If you don't know any better, maybe. Those pieces of garbage are definitely not what I'm going to use in my kitchen."

She pinched the bridge of her nose. "Hayden, can you just be straight with me? How much are we talking here?"

He brushed off some flour from his sleeve. "Probably close to ten grand."

Cadence's jaw nearly hit the floor. "What? First those stupid truffles, now a ten-thousand-dollar knife set? Holy cow. What next? A hundred-thousand-dollar fridge?"

Hayden looked alert. "What are the specs on it?"

This time she gave in and let her eyes roll toward the ceiling before coming back down. "Heaven help me."

HAYDEN BIT THE INSIDE of his cheek to keep from laughing at Cadence's exasperation. Seeing her this morning with her cheeks flushed and pieces of hair falling out of her bun was a treat he hadn't expected. But when he'd gotten a notice that his favorite knife maker had a new set out, he had grabbed the excuse to come talk to her.

He chose to ignore the fact that he could have just sent her a text or email rather than seeing her in person.

Ticking her off is so much more fun face to face. That's all. That and the fact that I have a challenge to win. Although, making her angry probably isn't the best way to get her to go on a date with me. He cleared his throat. "So, Cadence. I've been thinking," he said in a silky voice.

She kept her head down as she wrote something on a piece of paper, clearly trying to ignore him. "What? That you'd now like to buy some exotic duck found only in marsh lands of South Asia?"

"Funny." Hayden kept a straight face. "I'm laughing... on the inside."

The edge of her lip twitched and Hayden gave himself a mental high five.

"Are you going to say what you were thinking? Or am I going to have to guess again?" She paused in her task, folded her hands and turned her attention toward him.

Hayden shrugged. "I've been thinking that you owe me a date. I mean, you were, after all, the one who issued that little challenge and we both know I never give up, so," he spread his hands wide, "it would be easiest to just save ourselves the trouble."

Cadence froze.

Hayden waited, but Cadence still didn't move. Finally, he raised his eyebrows and tilted his head. "Cadence? Are you going to say anything or should I just plan on you picking me up at seven?"

His words must have jolted her out of her stupor, because she scowled and shook her head, muttering something about how it had been the weirdest day.

Hayden tapped his lips. "Hmm... guess that means I get to pick. How about-"

"No!" Cadence blurted, then blushed bright pink. "I'm not some little trophy at the end of the race, Hayden. I'm not going out with you just because you have a competitive side."

"Maybe I'm asking because I genuinely want to go out with you."

Cadence snorted. "That'll be the day."

Even though he knew it was coming, Hayden still found himself smarting from the rejection. "Oh yeah? And just why is that?"

Cadence sighed and rubbed her temples. "One, we fight. All the time. And I have no reason to believe that eating dinner together would stop that reaction to each other's company. Two, you're one of my bosses. It would be unprofessional for us to date." Cadence stopped and looked at him expectantly.

"Hayden, did you hear me?"

"Oh yeah, I heard. I'm just still waiting to hear an actual legitimate reason."

"What do you mean? Those are legitimate reasons." Cadence threw her hands in the air.

"Uh, no. Those are excuses. And neither one of them are any good." He tisked. "At least use a little imagination next time." He put his hand up when Cadence would have spoken again. "One, maybe you're just always hangry and that's why we don't get along. In which case," he pointed to himself, "I'm a chef. I can fix hangry. Problem solved."

Cadence barked out a laugh then quickly covered her mouth with her hands.

Ah, two victories in one day. "Reason number two, my brother just married a woman who worked," he held up his finger, "who still works for him. Obviously, people date in a workplace quite successfully when they want to."

He stopped speaking and stared intently at the woman across from him. He noticed the pulse point in her neck speed up as she stared back. The air began to get heavy and nearly crackled with anticipation. Her open gaze said she was just as affected as he was and the thought sent Hayden's attraction into overdrive. Just as he was about to jump across the desk and lay one on her, Cadence blurted out. "I already have a date!"

Hayden felt as if he had been slapped. His eyes widened, and he plopped back in his seat. It felt as if he'd been socked in the gut. *She has a date? How did I not know she's been dating someone? And why in the world does it bother me? I was only asking her out to win the competition. Wasn't I?* "I didn't know you were dating someone."

"Well," Cadence cleared her throat. "I'm not *dating* anyone. I just have a date. It's actually a fairly recent development. Someone I met a while ago. So, it wouldn't really be fair for me to go out with you when I already promised to go out with him."

"I see." Oh, Hayden saw all right. He could see that she was desperately trying to get rid of him and it made him want to dig in his heels even more. *This game just got kicked up a notch. Ha! We'll see who comes out the winner.*

He stood and walked to the door. "Anyone I know?" he asked cooly, glancing at Cadence from under his eyelashes.

"Uh, no. He's another accountant I met online."

Hayden pursed his lips and nodded. "Sounds exhilarating."

Cadence gave him a look. "Don't you need to go back to the kitchen or something? You might need to make sure they're chopping every itty, bitty vegetable to exact lengths."

Hayden pointed a finger. "You mock, but if your salad came out in weird sized chunks, I'd be the first to hear about it."

"Whatever," Cadence mumbled. "Better hurry, I think I smell something burning."

"Who knew the boring numbers lady had a sense of humor?" Hayden shot back before walking swiftly out the door, leaving a sputtering Cadence behind.

The idea that Cadence would go out with another man and not him irked Hayden to no end. "Just who is this guy? Another accountant?" He scoffed as he walked down the hall. "Bet he can't make that fire flash in her eyes the way I can. In fact," he grinned, "maybe I just need to convince Cadence going out with someone else is a waste of time."

Hayden chose not to examine too closely why he was willing to put in such an effort to get her attention. *I'm just a competitive guy.* He assured himself. *I learned long ago that you either win or you get run over. I choose to win.*

CHAPTER 7

Cadence finished swiping the lipstick on her mouth and studied herself in the mirror. For the first time in a year, she was headed out on a date. *And NOT with Hayden Truman.* She looked heavenward and shook her head. "As if I would ever date that richy jerk." *Even if he is attractive and surprisingly funny when he wants to be.* She shoved the prick at her conscience aside. "I couldn't go on a date with him. Someone has to protect our jobs," she said in an effort to convince herself of its truth. But if she was being honest with herself, she knew she was really protecting herself. *Hayden is everything I'm attracted to and everything I shouldn't have. After all, I've learned what powerful, rich men do with their lives.* "And I want no part of it," she finished out loud.

Shoving her attraction to the brooding chef aside, she focused on who she was meeting for dinner. Oliver Stevenson was the exact opposite of the previous men in her life. His face was average and his clothes off the rack, but he was intelligent, and helpful. "And that is more important than looks," she reminded herself.

Grabbing her purse, Cadence slipped out the door and got into her car. Not long after she had gotten the job at the castle, Cadence had traded in the sports car her father had given her for a sensible sedan and tonight she was even more grateful that she wouldn't come off as a rich, society girl when she met up with her date.

Her cabin was only moments from the castle, but Cadence hadn't wanted to walk in her heels, and she hadn't wanted Oliver to know where she lived just yet. After giving her permission to pick the place they ate at, Oliver had later texted and asked if they could eat at the resort. Unable to come up with a valid reason to say no, Cadence had agreed. "I couldn't exactly tell him that I didn't want to see Hayden," she grumbled. *Hayden.* Cadence pinched her lips. *I will not think of him tonight. He only sees me as a challenge because I don't fall at his feet like all the other girls do.*

"Cadence?" Oliver's pinched voice carried across the parking lot.

"Oliver!" Cadence smiled as she stood from her car. She pressed the lock on her keyring and walked over to where he waited. "Good to see you." Cadence stuck out her hand and Oliver met it. His hand was slightly clammy and his shake weak. *Doesn't matter. He's probably just nervous.*

"Good to see you, too." Oliver let go of her hand and turned to sneeze. "Sorry." He sniffed, grabbing a handkerchief out of his back pocket. "Allergies." He blew his nose loudly, folded the fabric and put it back in his pocket.

Eww. Cadence shook her head. "Are you ready to eat?"

Oliver turned and eyed the resort. "This place is a little fancier than I'm used to, but I'm sure I'll be able to find something."

Then why did you pick it? Cadence pasted a smile on to hide her disappointment at his attitude. "They have delicious food. I'm sure you'll love it."

She led the way as they wound through the cars up to the front entrance. "Hi, Bethany. I have a reservation for two," Cadence said to the hostess.

"Hello, Ms. Everwood. You look gorgeous tonight!" The young blonde woman said. "Got a hot-" Her eyes shot over Cadence's shoulder. "Oh. I mean. Um... let me just find that table for you."

Cadence's shoulders dropped a little, and she fought the desire to sigh. *He is exactly what you should be looking for. Just ignore her.* "Thank you," she said politely.

Oliver sneezed again behind her and she couldn't help but cringe when she heard him wipe his nose on the same handkerchief.

"Right this way, Ms. Everwood." Bethany turned and guided the two of them into the lush dining room. "Will this table do?" The hostess put her hand toward a small table off to the side with a glowing candle and a single rose in the center.

"This is great, thank you," Cadence answered when it was clear Oliver wasn't going to speak. His eyes were busy roaming over the dining hall, but instead of looking awed, he looked speculative.

I'm probably just reading him wrong. The restaurant is definitely impressive, especially if you haven't seen it before. Cadence stood and waited for Oliver to notice her and pull back her chair, but he simply wandered over to his own and sank down, his gaze still stuck on the chandelier. Cadence frowned and her eyes darted to Bethany, who was waiting to present them with the menus and wine list.

Bethany's face scrunched up, and she shrugged. Raising her eyebrows, Cadence gave an agreeing nod, then pulled out her own chair.

"Today's special is on the front and the wine selection on the back." Bethany clasped her hands in front of her. "Your waitress will be by shortly."

"Thank you," Cadence said with a smile then turned back to her date. Oliver was now studying the menu with a frown. Cadence waited, but he never looked up, so she delicately cleared her throat.

Oliver's eyes and brows jerked up. "Did you need something?"

"No... just wondering what you thought of the place." *Nice easy conversation.*

Oliver grunted and set down his menu. "I think they went over the top with everything."

Wait, what? Cadence felt her defenses rising. "What do you mean?"

"Well, like that chandelier." Oliver pointed toward the object. "Why would you spend so much money on something just for decoration? It's ridiculous." He shook his head. "It's nothing but a show of power."

"Oh, I thought it was beautiful." Cadence tried to smooth over the situation.

"Yeah, a woman would. They don't think about things like cost. Just spend, spend, spend."

"Excuse me?" *Where is this coming from? And why did I never see it when we chatted before? Ugh. Probably because we were always talking about work related things.*

Oliver held up a finger before blowing his nose again. "Women aren't as good with their money as men are. I mean, it's nothing personal." He smiled. "But women aren't savers. They don't know how to build a nest egg. They get too caught up in the next shiny thing."

Oh, no he didn't. It took every ounce of self control Cadence had not to blow her top at the sorry, little man in front of her. "I'm not sure if you remember that you're speaking to another accountant. I have a Masters in finance and you think I don't know about money?"

"Yeah, you're degree is great. But I'll bet if we compared bank accounts we would find that most of yours has gone toward that hair and those shoes." He waved his arm at her. "While mine is growing because I don't spend it on frivolous things."

"My bank account is none of your business, Oliver," Cadence said as calmly as possible.

Oliver tried to smirk, but it was ruined by another gigantic sneeze. "Exactly," he sniffed and wiped his nose, "my point."

Why does fate hate me? He was supposed to be the exact opposite of men like my father and Ryan. Is there no happy medium?

HAYDEN STOOD BACK WITH his arms crossed over his large chest and surveyed the bustling kitchen. Pride rumbled through him as he watched everything run like clockwork. *I might be known as a jerk, but I get things done and I get them done right.*

Running his own restaurant was a dream come true. He had thought it would take years to get this far. Then, after getting black-balled in New York, he assumed his dream was over. *Finding that trea-*

sure has been the best thing that could have happened to us. He frowned. *Well, mostly anyway.* The media firestorm had taken the brothers by surprise and consistently made life difficult. Hayden and his brothers had been dubbed the "Overnight Billionaire Bachelors". A name that caused Hayden to snort, Eli to frown and Nelson, the youngest, to rub his hands in glee. Luckily, their twin sisters, Teagan and Laken, were in college at the time of the discovery and hadn't been hounded the same way the men were. *Although, Eli said we should bring them out here and give them jobs.* He frowned. *We'll probably have to start fighting off guys as well as women.* Hayden rolled his eyes.

The three brothers had used the money to completely remodel the old, crumbling castle they had originally purchased and turn it into a five star resort. Eli, the oldest, took care of the hospitality side. Nelson ran a successful outdoor adventures business, using the resort guests, and Hayden had finally been able to see his dream come to fruition. He had built an in-house restaurant in the castle and it had been a smashing success from the time it opened. He had every intention of eventually gaining enough attention to bring over the right people so he could shoot for the elusive three Michelin Star ranking that all new chefs dream about.

Take that, Joyce. Hayden thought towards the woman who had been the instigator of his fall-out in New York. He found his lip curling as he thought of the pushy, seductress who wouldn't take no for an answer.

He had run from New York with his tail between his legs, but had come out on top. Contentment mixed with the pride as Hayden continued to survey his domain. He ran a tight ship and demanded the best of everyone who worked for him. Some people called him mean and grouchy, but Hayden preferred to think of himself as driven or passionate. *If they can't take the heat, they can get out of the kitchen.*

Seeing no problems with his well-oiled machine, Hayden decided to have a walk through the dining room. *Guess I can thank Joyce for teaching me one thing. Taking care of the customers is just as important as taking care of the kitchen.* He snorted.

With one last glance at his kitchen, he pushed through the door that led to the dining space.

Slowly, he sauntered through the tables. Every once in a while, he stopped to check on someone's food. Several times, he was called over and Hayden took the opportunity to chat with repeat diners he had come to know over the last year since they opened.

"Hayden, my boy! How are you this evening?" A booming voice caught Hayden's attention, and he turned with a smile on his face.

"Victor!" Hayden strode over to the table. "How are you and the lovely Ms. Gardner this evening?" Hayden picked up Julia's soft, wrinkled hand and kissed the back of it.

"Oh, you," Julia tittered, her cheeks turning pink.

Victor's belly shook as he chuckled. "We're here, so of course, we're doing well. How goes the restaurant business?" He looked around. "From the looks of it, you're in fine shape."

Hayden grinned and nodded. "Things couldn't be better. We seem to get busier every night," he stated proudly.

"Glad to hear it, glad to hear it."

"How have you enjoyed your meal this evening?" Hayden glanced at their near empty plates. "Did you try something new tonight?"

"I always think I will, but I always end up going straight back to the filet. It's amazing," Julia gushed.

Hayden nodded his thanks and turned his attention to Victor.

"Same here. I just can't pull myself away from that Wagyu steak you make." He patted his stomach. "Perfection, every time." His eyes twinkled as he leaned forward. "My compliments to the chef," he said then laughed at his own joke.

Hayden grinned. "I'll pass the message along," he recited in response to the joke Victor told him every time they came in. "I'm glad to hear everything is satisfactory." He clapped Victor on the shoulder and made ready to leave them to the plates when Julia interrupted him.

"Hayden," she said quietly, then gestured for him to come closer. Once Hayden had leaned down, she whispered in his ear. "I think you should go check on the table straight across from us against the wall."

Hayden started to jerk his head up, but Julia pulled on his shirt. "No. Don't look, or she'll know I'm talking about her."

Hayden had to hold in his eye roll. "Ms. Gardner, are you still trying to set me up?"

Julia frowned at him "Nonsense."

Hayden raised an eyebrow.

"Well, maybe. But that's neither here nor there. There is a beautiful woman over there who does not appear to be enjoying her date." Julia winked. "Perhaps you could just check to make sure her food is okay. Nothing wrong with that, right?"

"Julia, leave the boy alone. He's got plenty of time to get himself leg shackled," Victor said with a grin.

An imperious eyebrow shot up. "Leg shackled? You consider yourself in bondage, Mr. Gardner?" Julia's tone was crisp and cold.

Victor grinned and leaned forward to capture his wife's hand. "Of course! You stole my heart from the moment I saw you. You've been my captor ever since."

Hayden chuckled as he watched the blush creep back into the older woman's cheeks. "You, Dear, are ridiculous," Julia scolded half heartedly.

"Ridiculously in love with you," Victor shot back.

While Julia giggled like a schoolgirl, Victor glanced at Hayden and winked. "The girl she's talking about really is pretty, you should introduce yourself and knock that other guy to the curb," Victor whispered with a mischievous smirk.

"So, noted," Hayden said. "You two have a nice evening." With a nod, Hayden walked away from the table, intending to go back toward the kitchen. Out of curiosity, he glanced sideways toward the table Julia had been referring to and stopped in his tracks.

Cadence. Hayden's eyes darted to her companion. *And who the heck is that? Is that her date?* A slim man of medium height in a rumpled suit sat across from Cadence, a placating expression on his face as he waved his hand around and talked. After a moment, he sneezed, pulled a kerchief out of his pocket and blew his nose, then proceeded to put the cloth back. "You've got to be kidding me." Hayden scrunched up his face and looked to see what Cadence was doing. Instead of looking grossed out, she appeared angry. A slow grin grew on Hayden's face. *Well, well, well. Cadence looks about ready to lose it. Maybe as a friend I should go make sure she doesn't do anything she will regret.*

Adding a little swagger to his step, Hayden worked his way over to Cadence's table.

"Your comments are sexist and I won't-" Cadence's eyes jerked up. "Hayden! What are you-?" She closed her eyes and slumped ever so slightly. Straightening herself, she plastered a fake smile on. "Hello, Mr. Truman. How are you this evening?"

Her date jerked upright. "Mr. Truman?" He looked at Hayden with wide, excited eyes then back at Cadence. "As in one of the owners of this resort, Mr. Truman?"

Cadence frowned. "Um, yes. This is Hayden Truman, he owns and runs the restaurant. I suppose I should have introduced him as Chef Truman."

"Oh," he slumped back a little. At Cadence's confused expression, he explained. "I was hoping you were referring to Eli. The oldest brother."

Hayden spread his legs and crossed his arms, knowing the stance caused him to look bigger and more intimidating. It was a tactic he had perfected as a teenager. "Really? And why is that?"

The man seemed to shrink in his seat a little. "Well, um," he grabbed his handkerchief and dabbed his forehead with it, "I was hoping to talk to him about his retirement plan. I understand he runs the money making part of the resort and I have some ideas for him."

Hayden caught the disgusted look on Cadence's face before it shifted into horror. "You can't be serious."

The man looked affronted at Cadence's comment. "Of course I am. You knew I worked in retirement accounts. Why wouldn't I be interested in talking to him about them?"

"So you only asked me out because you wanted to talk to Mr. Truman?"

Hayden's head was bouncing between the two like a ping-pong ball. He found he wasn't even offended by the man's insults and lack of tact. It was proving to be too entertaining, he found he wasn't even sorry that Cadence's date was turning out to be such a loser. *Ooh, careful buddy. You're in dangerous waters now.*

"Now, I didn't say that." The man wiped his forehead again.

I sure hope all that snot has dried. The guy is a walking health code violation.

"But if we had run into him, it would have been a happy coincidence."

Nope. Not good enough. She'll tear you to shreds.

To Hayden's surprise, Cadence's face fell, and she closed her eyes for a few moments. When she opened them, she appeared calm and in control.

"Thank you for your invitation tonight, Oliver, but I think it best if I go home." Standing up before anyone else could react, Cadence swiftly left the dining room.

Wait. What? Where's the passion and fire that she hits me with? Hayden's eyes quickly looked down at the man Cadence had called Oliver.

Oliver's face had turned a mottled shade of red and he was gripping his handkerchief like a lifeline. "Should have known better than ask out a woman like her," he muttered before shoving his chair back.

"Wait a minute." Hayden put his hand on the man's chest and stopped his forward progress. "What do you mean a woman like her?"

"Rich women always think they're too good for everyone else." Oliver sniffed and brushed off the front of his shirt where Hayden had touched him. "They expect compliments and flattery rather than living in the real world. It doesn't occur to them that some of us have to work for a living."

"Rich women? You're talking about Cadence?" Hayden scoffed. "Boy, you're roasting the wrong pig. Cadence is paid well for her job here, but she's not wealthy. I don't know where you got that idea."

Oliver shook his head and sneered at Hayden. "Did you see those shoes she was wearing? They cost more than most people make in a month. Where exactly does she get off buying things like that unless she's got money, hmm?"

I let it go the first time, but he's crossed a line now. Hayden glanced around to see how much attention they had garnered during their exchange. To his disgust a fair amount of the customers were eavesdropping on their conversation. *Customer or not, he's gotta go. But keep it cool, Hay. You're the owner now.* "I believe you've said enough to show that you have no idea what you're talking about. Now, either get out or I'll put you out."

"Gladly." Oliver marched past Hayden. "Like I'd pay to eat anything you made, anyway," he shot over his shoulder.

Hayden growled and took a step in the man's direction. With a short squeal, Oliver scurried the rest of the way out of the castle. "Good riddance," Hayden grumbled.

A few snickers could be heard around the room, but otherwise no one said anything about the incident. *Guess I lucked out tonight.*

Hayden lifted his chin at one of the waiters in the area.

The young man hurried over. "Is everything all right, Sir?"

Hayden cleared his throat. "These guests have left. Clean up their waters and reset the table."

The waiter nodded. "Yes, Sir. Thank you, Sir."

"Oh, and Evan?"

The waiter paused in his cleaning and looked up at Hayden.

"Make sure table thirteen gets a couple of desserts on the house."

Evan nodded and Hayden took off to the kitchens. "James!" He bellowed for his Sous Chef as he burst through the revolving doors.

"Yes, Chef?" James' blond head popped up from one of the prep areas.

"I have to run out for the rest of the evening. Take over and close up."

"Yes, Chef."

"And get me a double helping of the lava cake with two scoops of vanilla."

"Yes, Chef."

Minutes later, Hayden held a styrofoam container in his hands as he walked to Cadence's cabin. *Time to work on that challenge.*

CHAPTER 8

Cadence slammed her cabin door, dropped her purse and jacket, and let herself fall onto the couch. Leaning forward, she put her head in her hands. "Stupid, stupid, stupid," she muttered. "I can't believe I went out with such a... sexist jerk." She dragged in a few deep breaths and did her best to calm down her racing heart.

"He only asked me out so he could get to Eli. Who does that?" she asked the empty cabin. The old feelings of hurt and betrayal from Ryan's actions slammed back into her chest, nearly taking her breath away. *And who seems to have trouble attracting men who aren't actually interested in her as a person? Me. That's who.*

"Am I just not worthy of being loved?" Cadence's voice was small and pitiful, but it matched how she felt. She might not have had romantic feelings for Oliver, but knowing she was only a means to an end still stung.

Her stomach growled, snapping her out of her pity party, and she groaned. "Great. Not only did I embarrass myself to high heaven, but I lost my only good meal of the day to boot."

When her stomach growled again, she debated trying to cook something, but between her lack of culinary skills and her exhaustion, the idea was far from appealing.

With a sigh, she rose and walked over to her cupboards. Pulling open the bottom drawer, she studied the collection of meal replacement bars she had accumulated. "Bleh. Nothing sounds good," she grumbled. "I'm so tired of sawdust."

Bang, bang, bang.

Cadence jumped at the sound. "Who in the world would be coming at this time of night? Oh my word, Oliver better not have followed me." With a frown, she walked over and opened the door.

"Hayden?" Cadence's earlier frustration came pouring back. She folded her arms over her chest. "What are you doing here?"

Hayden smirked and held out a styrofoam box. "I brought chocolate."

Cadence's heart took off in a gallop. *He did what? Who is this guy?* "Hayden..." She shook her head, and a smile pulled on her lips. "That's actually really-"

"I thought you might need a boost after picking such a loser of a date."

The words brought Cadence's warm, fuzzy feelings to a screeching halt. "And here I had the mistaken impression that you might actually be a nice guy." She put a hand on her cocked hip and raised an eyebrow.

Hayden's smirk stay in place while he stepped into her space. He smelled of spices and homemade bread and Cadence had to hold her breath to keep from sucking in a lungful. "Who says I'm not a nice guy?"

"Every kitchen worker who has run out of your office crying," she stated bluntly.

Hayden snorted. "It's not my fault they couldn't hack it. I run my kitchen a certain way. People have to either keep up or get out."

"Or maybe you're just a jerk. No one is perfect, including you," she retorted.

Hayden's enticing lips twitched and Cadence found her eyes drawn to them. "No person is perfect, but they *can* do certain things perfectly. My *kitchen* will be perfect. There might be some wimps who cry foul, but those who survive come out better in the end."

Cadence narrowed her eyes. "Maybe Eli was right."

Something flashed through Hayden's eyes, but it was too quick for Cadence to catch. "About what?"

"He once told me you weren't a jerk, you were simply passionate. And then explained that that was why you have no filter."

Hayden shrugged and tilted his head. "I call it like it is. You can't get better if you don't know what you're doing wrong."

Cadence opened her mouth to argue, but her stomach interrupted their interlude.

Hayden glanced down and back up. "Looks like I'm a nice guy after all."

Cadence rolled her eyes. "Whatever." She grabbed the container and went to close the door. "Thank you," she said as she pushed it closed, her good manners winning out.

The door stopped before it latched and Hayden shoved it back open before making his way into the cabin. "You look like you could use some company."

"I prefer pleasant companionship while I eat." Cadence grabbed a fork and started walking toward the couch, knowing she wouldn't be able to physically push him out. *Maybe a few well-placed words will get rid of him and that delicious scent.* "Namely, my own."

Hayden ignored her jab and wandered around the tiny home, looking at all the personal touches she had put around. He picked up a picture she kept on an accent table and Cadence stiffened. "Your parents?" he guessed.

She nodded stiffly, then forced her attention back onto her food. She nearly groaned when she took a bite of the still warm cake. *So much better than a protein bar.*

"Where do they live?"

Cadence's eyes glanced up at him, then back down. "California."

"Any siblings?" Hayden continued walking around her space.

"No," she said curtly.

"That had to be lonely, no wonder you're used to your own company."

Cadence shrugged. "Obviously, I survived just fine."

Hayden wandered into the kitchen and looked at the open drawer. "What's this?" He bent down and then stood, frowning. He held one of her protein bars in his hand. "You actually eat this garbage?"

Cadence rolled her eyes. "They're not that bad. Not all of us are trained chefs, you know."

He paused from where he had been dropping the bar in the trash can. "Everyone can cook better than those stupid things."

Cadence snorted before she realized what she was doing. In no time she felt her neck and cheeks heat up. *Ignore, ignore, ignore.*

"Cadence?"

She kept her head down. She could tell he was walking toward her, but she did her best to ignore him and focus on her dessert. When he sat down beside her, ignoring him became all but impossible.

"Cadi?" He teased softly as he slid onto the cushion next to her.

She jerked up. "What did you call me?" *Anger. Yes. Focus on the anger, not his face, voice or how he smells.*

Hayden grinned. "Cadi sounds much less stuffy than Cadence."

"But my name is Cadence, not Cadi."

Hayden rolled his eyes and leaned back on the couch. "That's why it's called a nickname. Now, back to the cooking thing."

"No," she burst out.

"No, you can't cook? Or no, you don't want to talk about it?"

"I don't want to talk about it," she said frostily. *I'm starting new here. Not dredging up my childhood.*

"Have we finally found something the inestimable Cadence Everwood can't do?"

Cadence dropped her dessert on the coffee table, jumped up from the couch and put her hands on her hips. "What is that supposed to mean?"

Hayden spread his arms on the back of the couch on either side of himself. "You're an independent, educated, beautiful woman, Cadi.

You appear to excel at everything, it's nice to know you're human just like the rest of us."

Cadence did her best to hide the warm fuzzies shooting through her from his compliment, instead she frowned and crossed her arms. "Oh? And what about you? Are you human as well?"

Hayden stood and pushed himself right into her space.

Cadence gasped and tried to back up, but Hayden followed her.

"Oh, I'm human, Cadi. There are plenty of people who say my drive for perfection is a flaw." His voice was deep and husky. This close she could see that his dark eyes were actually brown even though from a distance they appeared as black as his hair. *Whoa...*

Cadence gulped, but she pushed herself to stand her ground. "Striving for perfection isn't necessarily a flaw. It's how you choose to get there that can be the problem."

Hayden tilted his head and studied her. "Really? And how am I choosing to get there?"

The room felt too hot and claustrophobic, but Cadence refused to let Hayden win. *Must be another one of my flaws.* "The ability to bully people is not something someone would write on a resume."

One side of Hayden's mouth pulled up. "I see. What would you have me do, then? Tell everyone they're winners no matter what they do? Give participation trophies?"

Cadence shook her head. "You can still achieve perfection by using kindness. An added bonus is that the people still like you afterwards."

Hayden narrowed his eyes. "You want me to be more kind." It was a statement not a question, but Cadence answered anyway.

"You asked what flaw made you human. I simply answered."

Hayden grabbed her hand and put it on his chest. His very warm, muscular chest. Every muscle in Cadence's body stiffened. *What is he doing?*

"I think it's pretty easy to tell that I'm human, don't you think, Cadi?"

Cadence didn't answer. Her wide eyes had traveled from where he held her hand captive to his dark, bottomless pools of dark chocolate.

Slowly, Hayden wrapped his other hand around her waist, pulling her body into his. He leaned down until his lips were against her ear. "If being nice will make me more human, then by all means, I'll do something nice."

Cadence couldn't breathe. The electricity snapping in the air had paralyzed every part of her, including her lungs. Hayden's overwhelming presence was suffocating, and she didn't have enough control over her body to pull away. *I shouldn't do this. I know how this will end. Men like him can't be trusted. So why can't I walk away?*

Hayden nipped at her earlobe and Cadence sucked in a much needed gasp of air.

"Our biggest flaws can become our greatest strengths," Hayden murmured against her skin as he worked his way across her cheek. "So out of the *kindness* of my heart, I'm going to teach you to cook."

His lips had reached hers and they hovered so close Cadence could feel the heat of his breath gently caressing her face.

"How's that for kind?" He whispered.

Cadence still didn't answer. Her mind was fighting desperately to catch up with his words, but being so close to him was throwing off her thought processes.

"Say yes, Cadi," Hayden urged.

"Y-yes," she parroted without conscious thought.

"Good girl," he murmured before closing the gap between them and pressing his lips to hers.

Cadence's eyes fluttered closed, and she took in a long breath through her nose. All the tension surrounding them burst to life, and it felt as if fireworks were exploding in the cabin. Warmth and excitement rushed through Cadence and she found herself responding to him easily, naturally, as if she were where she belonged. Her hands crawled up his shoulders and wrapped themselves around his neck.

With his hand now free, Hayden took the opportunity to palm the back of her head and tilt her head so he could deepen the kiss. His dark stubble rubbed against the delicate skin around her lips and provided an exciting contrast to the softness of his masterful lips. *Eli was right... wait, no, I can't do this. No!* When her mind finally caught up with her actions, Cadence yanked herself out of his arms, gasping. Once out of his embrace, her body temperature plummeted and the urge to go back nearly drove her insane. Forcing herself to step further away, she put up a hand and bent over, breathing heavily. "Stop. We can't do this."

Hayden folded his arms and scowled. "Lessons start Monday, eight o'clock after the dinner rush, in the kitchens." Then he was gone.

"What? No!" Cadence rushed outside, but Hayden was nowhere to be seen. With a screech, she stormed back into her home.

"If he thinks I'm going to spend time with him so I can learn how to boil water, he's got another thing coming. I don't care how amazing his kissing is." Grabbing the rest of her cake, she slumped onto the couch. "Or his chocolate." Stuffing a massive bite in her mouth, she turned on a movie, determined to leave Hayden and her conflicting feelings behind.

Just as she was settling in, her phone buzzed. Reluctantly, she grabbed it and looked at the text.

I'm sorry about tonight. I was nervous and said things I shouldn't have. I really would like to take you on a date. No Trumans involved. Can I please have another chance?

Cadence scrunched her nose. Her first instinct was to tell Oliver 'no', after all, the night had been a disaster long before Hayden showed up. Then she thought of Hayden and his overbearing personality and texted before she could think better of it.

That's fine. When works for you?

How about next Friday?

Sounds good.

Oliver sent a thumbs up and the conversation ended.

"Ha." Cadence threw her phone on the couch. "Take that, Hayden." With an evil cackle, she stuffed another bite of dessert in.

WAY TO GO, IDIOT. Hayden shook his head as he headed back to the resort so he could grab his car. "You're lucky she didn't slap you." *No matter that it was amazing.*

After jumping into his low-slung sports car, he revved the engine and took off for his home. His fingers thrummed on the steering wheel as he worked his way along the dark forest road that led to the three rustic mansions the brothers had built for themselves while they were renovating the castle.

After a few minutes he pulled into his six-car garage and went inside. He didn't bother flipping on any lights as he headed to the master bedroom. Walking into his bathroom, he began to get ready for bed. His movements were jerky and agitated.

Pausing in his attempt to put toothpaste on his toothbrush, he rested his hands on either side of the sink and looked at himself in the mirror. "You are being ridiculous," he scolded his reflection.

He couldn't get the kiss with Cadence out of his head. How soft she felt, how sweet she smelled and how fantastic she tasted. It was like having a bite of the ultimate dessert and knowing you would never be able to replicate it again.

Hayden hung his head and took a deep breath. "This attraction is getting out of hand and I feel like I'm playing with fire." He gave a self-deprecating laugh. "And the best part is she's not even interested. The first woman I can't shake and she chooses to go out with *Oliver*," Hayden sneered.

The thought of the rude man brought a little fire back to Hayden's belly, and he pulled himself up right. "This isn't about anything except winning," he spoke to the mirror again. "You've never lost a challenge and you're not about to start now. If you can learn to flambé without melting ice cream, you can get Cadence to go on a date with you. And if being kind is the way to do that, then you'll be kind." He nodded his head. "By teaching her how to cook. It's as simple as whisk, bake, enjoy."

And you will put that kiss as far out of your head as possible.

CHAPTER 9

In the wee hours of Monday morning, before the sun began to peek over the tree line, Hayden drug himself from his car, up the stairs and into his bed. The weekend had been one long, exhausting blur of cooking, shouting and schmoozing.

Normally, Hayden ran the dinner shift and left breakfast to one of his sous chefs, but several of his workers had been sick and Hayden had ended up spending the whole weekend in the kitchen to help keep up with the demand of the resort guests. Not only did his kitchen send out food to the restaurant, but there was an extra crew who catered to room service as well.

This weekend, nearly every room had been booked and the sheer number of requests had kept everyone on their toes.

With a groan, Hayden threw himself onto his king sized bed, burying his face in one of the pillows. "I need to hire more staff," he mumbled into the soft fabric.

After pulling off his shirt and shoes, Hayden curled into the blankets and was snoring within moments.

He awoke with a jerk many hours later. Scrubbing his hands over his face, he tried to figure out what had pulled him from a very enjoyable dream.

Bang. Bang. Bang.

"They're gonna smash the door down," Hayden grumbled. "Who in the world is it?"

"Hay!" Nelson shouted from the bottom of the stairs. "Where you at?"

"Heaven help me," Hayden moaned. *I don't have the patience for his smiling face right now.*

Nelson's stomping got louder as he worked his way up the stairs. "Geez, man. And I thought I slept in late sometimes."

"Go away." Hayden threw his arm over his eyes.

"Now why would I do that? I just found you."

Hayden could hear the smugness in Nelson's tone and it made him want to rip the smirk off his brother's face and shove it out the window. "So your mission is complete. Now, get out of here."

"You're like a hibernating bear. What's the matter? Been away from your food supply for too long?"

"Did you have an actual purpose in finding me, or were you just looking to make my life miserable?"

"Well, you have to admit, it's not that hard to make you miserable. I mean, your favorite food is raw fish. Which is so stupid. Why the heck did you have to go to cooking school to learn how to serve uncooked food?"

Hayden moaned and rolled out of bed. "One of these days, I'm going to break into your house and try some new techniques with my torch. Then you'll really know what I learned at culinary school."

"Any place that teaches you to wear weird hats and skirts is not the place for me. I prefer more manly pursuits, but, hey. Whatever floats your boat."

"For the millionth time, it's an apron, you uncultured swine," Hayden growled. His irritation rose a notch as he heard Nelson laughing while walking back down the stairs.

After splashing his face with cool water and putting on a shirt, Hayden padded down the stairs. He rolled his eyes when he found Nelson eating straight out of one of his plastic food containers.

"Just what was so important that you had to come wake me up and eat my leftovers?"

"Have you been online lately?" Nelson said around a mouthful of mashed potatoes.

Hayden yawned and walked to the cupboard to get a glass. "When would I have time for that? I've been working for the last forty-eight hours."

Nelson pulled his phone out of his back pocket, clicked a few buttons, then shoved it in Hayden's face.

"Knock it off," Hayden said darkly, grabbing the phone and putting it where he could see it properly.

After watching himself on the small screen, Hayden realized what was going on. "Crud. Someone recorded us?"

"Dude, someone always records us." Nelson stuffed another bite in his mouth. "Haven't you figured that out by now?"

Hayden threw the phone back and Nelson fumbled as he caught it.

"Hey, that's a new phone."

Hayden huffed and turned to fill his glass. "Is that what you wanted to show me?"

"Did you not catch that it's going viral? Apparently, people like seeing the big bad chef threaten to throw someone out of his restaurant. They're calling you some very interesting names in the comments."

"The guy was using Cadence in order to get to Eli. What was I supposed to do?" He froze. "Cadence... oh, crud. What time is it?"

Nelson frowned and glanced at his phone. "Six. Why?" A slow smile crept across his face. "Did you ask her on a date? Oh man, that woman is a ten! Like seriously, a ten. Totally not my type, I mean, she looks like she'd freak if she got a mosquito bite, but-"

"Nelson! Shut up!" Hayden glared at him.

"Ah," Nelson smirked. "Got it, you're putting down a claim." He put his hands up. "No biggie. Like I said, not my type."

Hayden scrubbed his hands down his face. "You are the world's biggest imbecile." *Six. Okay. I've still got two hours until I have to meet Cadence.*

"Uh, no. That'd be the guy whose video is running around making him look like an overbearing sasquatch."

"Dude! Everyone knows I'm mean. That's never been a secret. They've been saying junk about me ever since I got hired in New York."

Nelson pursed his lips and nodded. "True." He shrugged and stuffed his phone back in his pocket. "I let that PR dude, what's his bucket, Michael? -know about it, but if you don't care about your image, then hey, more power to ya."

"Fine. Are you done eating me out of house and home now?" Hayden grabbed the dish out of Nelson's hands and took it to the sink.

"Don't know. Give me ten minutes and we'll see." Nelson plopped down on one of the leather barstools in Hayden's large kitchen.

Hayden shook his head. "And here I thought you weren't a teenager anymore."

"Some of us know better than to grow up." Nelson grinned and pumped his eyebrows. "You and Eli have proven that all it does is make you grumpy."

Hayden couldn't help the bark of laughter that burst out of him.

"So, about you and Cadence..." Nelson leaned in.

"There is no me and Cadence," Hayden butted in.

Nelson tilted his head. "But you want there to be."

Hayden scrunched his face. "Says who?"

"Says the fact that you got all cranky about the guy who was mistreating her at the restaurant."

Hayden gave a deadpan expression. "That's common courtesy. No gentleman would treat a lady like that."

"Last I looked, you weren't a gentleman."

Hayden scowled. "I was raised with the same manners you were."

"Maybe so, but I learned them better." Nelson leaned back and rubbed a hand down his chest. "The ladies love me for it."

Hayden snorted.

"You on the other hand? You've got that dark," Nelson waved a hand in the air, "brooding thing going on. I've heard some women like it, especially on vampires, so there might be hope for you yet."

Hayden rolled his eyes and put his glass in the dishwasher. "I need to go shower. Is there anything else you need?"

Nelson stood and stretched. "Nope. I've done all the mischief I can for now. I'll leave you to your bubble bath, or whatever it is you skirt-wearing men do."

Hayden growled and took a step in Nelson's direction.

Nelson laughed as he hightailed it out of the kitchen and toward the front door. "Have fun on your little date! Don't do anything I wouldn't do!"

"Brothers..." Hayden grumbled. Turning, he stalked up the stairs to wash off before he headed back to the kitchens for Cadence's cooking lesson.

An hour later he jumped in his car and took off for the restaurant. Parking in the far back, he weaved his way through the other cars and walked inside.

"Chef!" James called out in surprise. "I didn't know you were coming in. Is everything okay?"

Hayden waved a hand at him. "Yeah. It's fine. I'm giving a cooking lesson. I'm going to be setting up in the back. So don't worry about me. Just keep things running."

"Yes, Chef." James nodded and went back to his work.

Hayden watched the flow of workers for a moment before nodding in satisfaction. Heading back to the walk-in, he grabbed the ingredients he would need in order to teach Cadence how to make pasta and cream sauce. "A perfect starter dish," he mumbled as he prepared his work table.

When he was finished, he glanced at his watch. "Ten minutes. Perfect."

Pulling out his phone, he scrolled through his social media pages while he waited. When he got bored, he glanced at his watch again. "She's late." Without thinking about it, he began to pace, glancing between his watch and the door every few seconds.

"Everything all right, Chef?" James walked over with a concerned expression on his face.

Hayden froze. "Uh, yeah." Heat traveled up his neck and he cleared his throat. "Everything's fine. I'm sure she'll be here soon."

James nodded and backed away. "Okay, Chef. Let me know if you need anything."

Hayden nodded stiffly. *Why the heck am I so worked up? So, she's a few minutes late, so what?* He glanced around the kitchen to the bustling workers. "I'd fire any of them if they were ten minutes late," he said with a scowl.

Shoving his feelings aside, he spent the next few minutes researching large, walk in fridges. "It would serve her right if I bought a new one," he growled.

When he glanced at his watch to see that she was now more than twenty minutes late, he knew he'd been stood up. Without a word, he cleaned up his area, ignoring the pitying and curious glances of his workers.

Once done, he stormed out of the kitchen and headed toward Cadence's office. *I'll check there first.*

Multiple knocks and a try at the knob proved she wasn't there. Clenching his jaw, Hayden burst out the front doors of the resort and took off for her cabin.

CADENCE GROANED AS she tried to contort her body into the same shape as the women on her computer screen. "Sheesh. Just goes to show you what too many nights of eating fast food and binging on shows will do to you."

A drop of sweat ran down the side of her face and dripped off her chin. *Ugh.* Breaking stance, she grabbed a towel and wiped her face. *Why do I torture myself like this?*

All weekend she had kept herself busy, doing her best to put Hayden and that world-changing kiss out of her head. And now, she was putting herself through her hardest yoga workout in order to keep from thinking about the fact that she was supposed to be at the kitchens having him teach her how to cook.

She snorted. "Maybe now he'll get the message he refused to hear," she grumbled. *Time to get back at it.*

"Let's go." Slowly, she eased her aching muscles back into the position the instructor was at. Just as Cadence got her hips off the ground, and her right arm at the correct angle, there was a loud banging at the door. "What in the-?"

Before she could call out, the door burst open.

Cadence screamed and collapsed in a heap on the floor. "Hayden!" she screeched. "What the heck are you doing?"

Hayden folded his arms over his chest and raised an eyebrow. "I was checking to make sure you weren't dead. Or maybe that your cabin was on fire. Those were the only reasons I could think of as to why you would so rudely stand me up."

Cadence's temper erupted instantly. "Rude? You think I'm the rude one? How about the fact that I said 'no' to your little lesson? Hmm? Isn't it rude not to listen when people give you answers? Or how about you busting into my private residence? I think rude fits in that situation as well."

Hayden tisked his tongue and shut the door, waltzing in as if he owned the place. "Cadi, Cadi, Cadi."

"Stop calling me that!" she hissed.

"Sometimes people are put into our paths to push us. To help us step outside of ourselves."

Cadence snorted. "And you think you're one of those people? Tell me, O Wise One, how exactly you're supposed to help me step outside of myself."

Hayden closed the distance between them. "I'm here to help you overcome your fear of cooking."

Cadence scrunched her face and tried not to breathe in his amazing smell. *Why does he always smell like fresh bread? Do they bottle that scent and sell it in a kitchen store? And here I am stinking of sweat and frozen lasagna. Soooo unfair.* "I'm not afraid of cooking, I just don't need your help." She stepped around him and took hold of the doorknob. "Now if you'll excuse me, I was in the middle of exercising."

Hayden turned to follow her progress, but didn't make a step to leave. "Prove it."

Cadence laughed. "What? Are we like five? Who says prove it anymore?"

"I believe I just did." Hayden smirked and put his hands on his hips.

"I don't have to prove anything to you. Now if you'll just-"

Hayden yawned and let himself fall on the couch. "I'm not sure I have the energy to make it back to my house. I think I'll just crash here."

"Hayden!" Cadence said through clenched teeth. "You are impossible!"

He closed his eyes. "Now that I think about it, I'm pretty hungry. Can you make me something?"

"Make your own thing! In your own house! In your own kitchen!" *Do not laugh, do not laugh. It will only encourage him.* She chewed the inside of her lip. She'd never seen Hayden so playful before and the sight of the man who struck fear into the hearts of kitchen workers everywhere acting like a little kid was cracking her up.

He reached a hand toward the kitchen. "I can't reach."

"Oh my gosh! Really?" Cadence walked over and grabbed Hayden's heavy arm. "Come on, you big oaf! Stop being such a baby."

Hayden gave a jerk and neatly pulled Cadence into his lap.

"Now who's the baby?" he asked with a grin.

"Oh!" Cadence knew her eyes were wide and her cheeks flushed. She used the palms of her hands against his shoulders to keep a little distance between them. "I guess I should have seen that coming," she said breathlessly.

Hayden took her hands and pushed them over his shoulders where they naturally curled around his neck. He pulled her in close, touching his nose to hers. "Admit you're scared of cooking and I will leave."

"I'm not scared," she whispered. *Pull away. Pull away. Why won't my body obey?*

Hayden shrugged and put his cheek on hers. "So you say," he whispered in her ear. "But I have no proof."

Finally, Cadence found a spark of frustration. Frustration at Hayden's pushing. Frustration at her body's attraction to him. Frustration at her nonexistent cooking skills. And she used that spark to keep herself from doing something stupid. *Like kissing the heck out of those lips.*

With a shove, she jumped out of his arms. "If I cook something will you leave?"

Hayden quirked an eyebrow at her sudden outburst. "You prove to me you can cook and I'll..." there was a slight hitch in his voice, "-leave you alone."

Her chest heaved for a few breaths and she glanced between him and the kitchen several times, debating whether or not she could pull it off.

"This shouldn't be that hard, Cadi," Hayden teased. "Either you can cook or you can't. I'm not asking for something fancy. How about pancakes?"

Cadence tried to keep from panicking. *Pancakes. They should be simple. Right? No biggie.* "Sure. I can handle that."

Hayden stood and swept an arm toward her kitchen.

Forcing her breathing to stay steady, Cadence took the three steps from the couch to her kitchen and began pulling open the cupboards. She banged around, not finding the box she was looking for. Finally, she turned to face Hayden. "So, it looks like I'm out of mix." *Or maybe*

I never bought any to begin with. "So we're going to have to do this another night." *Whew. Saved by the lack of groceries.*

Hayden's eyebrows shot up. "You don't need a mix. Make them from scratch."

Cadence's shoulders fell. "Scratch. Right." Pinching her lips, she turned back to the cupboards. She grabbed an old yellow bowl from one and set it on the counter. Resting her hands on either side of the bowl, she tapped her fingers in an impatient rhythm. *I have no idea how to make pancakes. What am I going to do?*

"I have a recipe memorized if you want..." Hayden trailed off.

Cadence spun. "Recipe! Yes! That would, uh, help. Thanks."

"Great. Grab your flour."

"Flour." She chewed her lip. "I'm uh, well, I guess I need to go grocery shopping because I'm out of flour."

Hayden coughed and put a fist to his mouth.

That sounded suspiciously like a laugh.

"Lucky you, I have all the ingredients at my house." Hayden started walking toward the door. "Come on," he called over his shoulder.

"What? Hayden, I'm not coming to your house to cook pancakes at nine o'clock at night."

He paused, his hand on the doorknob. "Why not?"

"I just said!" Cadence put her hands on her hips. "It's nine o'clock at night. And I'm in my yoga clothes."

"Better than getting nice clothes dirty." He opened the door. "Now are you coming, or am I going to have to keep bugging you about this?"

"Aargh! You are the most exasperating man! Do you ever give up?"

"Nope. It's why I'm so good at what I do."

"I don't want to go!" she whined.

"Wow. And you called me a baby?" He shrugged. "But it's okay, I can just camp out on your couch again. I'm super tired, anyway."

"No! You are not camping out on my couch." She pushed her hands into her hair and growled. "Fine! Fine. I'll make them at your house."

Grabbing a light jacket and pulling on her flip flops, she stormed out of her cabin.

Hayden came up behind her after closing the door.

"I forgot my keys, just a sec." Cadence started to turn back to the house.

"Nope." Hayden took hold of her elbow. "I'll drive us."

"How?" She looked around. "Your car isn't even here."

"It's at the resort. I walked from the restaurant."

"I can just meet you at your house, then."

"And give you the chance to no-show on me again?" Hayden grinned. "Not happening."

Cadence looked heavenward and shook her head before starting to walk. "I'm sorry. Did being stood up hurt your ego? Good thing it can take the hit." *This man brings out the worst in me. And yet I still want to kiss him. Why?*

"Sticks and stones, Cadi. Sticks and stones," came Hayden's amused voice behind her.

Cadence snapped her mouth shut. *I'm being just as childish as he is. Why? Why do I let him get to me like this?*

They walked in silence back to his sports car and drove to his mansion. He parked in the driveway. "Might as well keep the car out since I'll have to drive you back."

"Whatever." Cadence climbed out of the low car and marched up to his front door.

"Welcome to my humble abode," Hayden stated, flinging the door open for her to walk through.

Cadence snorted then slowed as she walked in. "It's beautiful," she breathed. Her eyes trailed along the log walls that rose for two stories. Their yellow color helped the large space look warm and inviting. Masculine, leather furniture surrounded a massive fireplace, above which was a TV the size of her car.

She shook her head. *Guess not all his toys are in the kitchen.*

"I can see it all the way from the kitchen," Hayden leaned in and whispered in her ear.

Holding in the shiver from his closeness was almost impossible, but Cadence definitely tried. She stepped away from his warmth. "Let's get this over with, shall we?"

She walked through the great room to the massive kitchen placed off to the side. Stainless steel appliances gleamed as if they were regularly polished. A butcher block was built into the countertop and copper pots and pans hung from a rack above the island.

"So this is what they call a chef's kitchen, huh?" Cadence shot him a cheesy grin over her shoulder.

"Oh, that's a good one. I've neeeever heard that one before."

Cadence couldn't help the small giggle that bubbled through her lips. *This reminds me of our kitchen at home. So large and shiny. And completely foreign.*

"Ready?"

Cadence jerked out of her memories. "Uh, yep. But I don't know where anything is."

"That's fine. I can direct you to anything you need."

Come on, Cadence. Put on your big girl panties and let's do this. "Right. Tell me that recipe."

"Flour, baking soda, salt, eggs, you know, the usual suspects."

"Uh, huh. The usual," Cadence murmured. *Why did I agree to this? I have no idea what I'm doing. There's no way I'm going to be able to fake it in front of him.*

There were several moments of silence before Hayden spoke up. "Are you going to get started?"

"Mm, hm," Cadence pinched her lips together.

"Well, then?" His lips were twitching and Cadence knew he knew she was lying.

He's just waiting for me to fail. To give in. Well, she straightened her shoulders. *I won't give him the satisfaction.* She put her hands on her hips. "How about a bowl?"

Hayden tilted his chin behind her. "Lower cupboard, to the right of the sink."

"Thank you," she said shortly before turning and grabbing what she needed. She set in on the counter. "Flour?"

Hayden had a small smile on his face. "Large stainless steel canister over there." He pointed to a long countertop. "It's the one marked flour."

"You're a regular comedian," Cadence muttered as she grabbed it and the sugar. *Pancakes are sweet, right? They must have sugar in them.*

Hayden nodded his approval with raised eyebrows as she walked back. "Very good," he said.

Ha! See? Just good common sense and I'll make it through this. "What else did you say was in the recipe?"

Hayden rattled off a list and directed Cadence to each item. Once she had them all lined up on the counter, she eyed them warily. *Okay, now what?* "Did... did your recipe have amounts in it?"

Hayden did that laugh/cough combo again before putting a serious expression back on his face. "Sure does."

"Stop making fun of me," she grumbled, "and just tell me what they are."

"Yes, Ma'am. You need three cups of flour."

Cup, cup, cup, cup, cup. She couldn't find anything so she turned to Hayden. "Where are your cups?"

"First drawer below the flour."

"Right." Cadence grabbed what she needed and came back. Hayden had settled himself in one of his cushy barstools and was leaning back with his arms folded.

One by one, Cadence did her best to measure out the recipe Hayden kept reciting for her. She tried not to think about what she looked like with flour on her nose and baking soda on her shirt. *Baking is just messy. No biggie. All cooks get dirty, right?*

"You need a couple of eggs." Hayden pointed out after she had finished putting in all the dry ingredients.

"'Kay…" *I've never cracked an egg before.* She picked up the oblong, white ball. Holding it in one hand, she tapped it lightly on the counter like she had seen chefs do on tv shows before. Nothing happened. *Hmm… must not have been hard enough.* She tapped a little harder. Still nothing. She scrunched up her face in frustration. The next time she hit down, the whole egg splattered under her hand. "Oh!" she cried, jumping back as the yolk spilled all over the counter.

Suddenly, a very distinct, warm presence was at her back. "We need to get that cleaned up so no one gets sick," he said softly.

With swift movements, Hayden wiped up the mess, dumping it all in the garbage and sanitizing the area.

Cadence watched him with wide eyes, unsure of how to help.

Once he was done, Hayden handed her another egg. "Try again."

Gulping, Cadence picked it up and faced the counter. She felt heat rush up her cheeks as Hayden stood at her back and held onto her hand which held the egg. "The trick is to tap the wide side, where the egg is at its weakest. We only want a crack, then our fingers can do the rest."

"Okay," Cadence squeaked, then cleared her throat. "I'm sorry about the mess. I guess I don't know my own strength."

Hayden's deep chuckle vibrated through her back and into her chest. *Oh my gosh, this is insane!*

Still holding her hand, Hayden guided her through getting the egg into the flour mixture. While they were working on the next one, he leaned into her ear again. "You can admit the truth at any time, you know."

Dang. I knew I couldn't pull it off. "Never," she whispered back, then bit her lip to hold back the smile wanting to spread across her face at Hayden's laugh.

After they were done with the eggs, Hayden stepped back and her body's cry at the loss of heat wasn't lost on Cadence. *I will not be disappointed. Nope. Nope. He's off limits. He's everything you left behind.*

"Would you like me to start preheating the pan?" Hayden asked as he walked over to another cupboard.

"Umm... sure. That'd be great. Thanks."

While Hayden moved around and started the burner, Cadence poured in the water he had mentioned and began to mix the batter. "Whoa," she murmured as some of it splashed over the side.

"You seem to be a very messy cook," Hayden said with a cough. "And yet I've never seen your kitchen messy at all."

"Maybe I'm just really good at cleaning up after myself," Cadence shot back.

Hayden nodded. "Or maybe you never use the kitchen."

"Sure I do. I used it just tonight."

"What did you make?"

"None of your business." *Making tea counts. The microwave is part of the kitchen.*

Hayden huffed. "So we're back to acting like children."

Cadence sighed and wiped a stray hair off her forehead. "No. Sorry."

"You've got-" Hayden pointed to his own forehead and swung his finger back and forth.

"Shoot." Cadence looked around for a towel but Hayden was quicker.

"Here. Let me." He walked up to her and Cadence backed away.

"No. I can do it. Just hand me the towel."

"Nope. You can't see it. You might miss some." His dark eyes twinkled with mirth and Cadence couldn't help but wish something could come of their mutual attraction to each other. *But one betrayal was plenty for me. I won't tempt fate with the same kind of man.*

"Whatever. Just get it." She squeezed her eyes shut and braced herself.

Hayden huffed a little laugh. "You look like you're bracing for impact. I'm pretty sure I have a softer touch than that."

Maybe so, but whenever you stand close, I have the most insane desire to burrow into your strong arms and never let go. "Sorry." She forced herself to relax, but the zing of electricity that always accompanied his touch still shot through her when he cleaned her face.

"All done, you can breathe now." He chuckled as he tossed the towel into a basket in the corner.

"Thanks," Cadence murmured, embarrassment flooding her cheeks.

"I'm starving, you gonna get those things cooked up soon?" Hayden asked as he plopped back down on the barstool.

"Didn't you eat dinner?" Cadence carried the bowl over to the hot pan.

"Nope."

"What?" Cadence spun around. "Why not?"

"I worked almost forty-eight hours straight at the restaurant. When I got home this morning, I fell into bed and didn't rise until this evening. I thought I'd be eating dinner when you had your cooking lesson." He pierced her with a hard glare.

"It was wrong of me to not show up. I'm sorry." She pointed a finger at him. "But you need to learn to take no for an answer."

"If I took no for an answer, I wouldn't have a beautiful woman in my kitchen attempting to cook pancakes."

Cadence rolled her eyes, but savored the warmth that rushed through her chest at his words. "Whatever." She turned back to the stove. Finding a spoon, she picked up some batter and plopped it onto the pan, where it immediately began to smoke. "Uh, what?"

"You should use some nonstick cooking spray. Or some butter."

"Oh. Yeah. Thanks." She searched for what he was talking about.

"Upper cupboard right in front of you."

"Right. Thanks. I guess I forgot."

Hayden snorted and muttered under his breath, but Cadence ignored him. She searched the drawers in front of her for something to pick up the pancake with, but couldn't see anything.

"Looking for this?" A spatula was pushed into her face.

"Oh!" She spun. "Do you enjoy scaring me?" *Sheesh. I didn't even hear him walk over here.*

He shrugged. "I wasn't trying to be sneaky. You were the one not paying attention."

"Fine." She snatched the utensil out of his hand. "Thank you," she snapped.

Hayden put his hands in the air and backed up. "Just helping out. We both know you need it."

Spinning around, she tried lifting the pancake out of the pan. After several unmentionable words were uttered and batter spilled over the edge, she finally managed to get the black, one-sided lump into the garbage.

"Let's try this again," she murmured. She picked up the pan and sprayed the non-stick oil at it. "Oh my gosh!" Cadence jumped back with when a flame shot up from the stove top. It went out as quickly as it came, but her heart rate wasn't so lucky.

"Whoa, there. I haven't lived here that long. I'd rather not go after the insurance quite yet." Hayden came up and snatched the aerosol can from her.

"What just happened?"

Taking the pan from her other hand, Hayden set it back on the burner. "You just sprayed an aerosol into an open flame." He looked over his shoulder. "Are you okay?"

She nodded, still shocked. "Uh, yeah. I've just, um, never had that happen before."

"Can't say the same. Any cook worth his salt has started a few fires in his time."

"Seriously?" Cadence grabbed his bicep without thinking. "Were you ever burned?"

"Nah, nothing major anyway. Now come on, I'm gonna faint if I don't eat soon."

Cadence shook her head and jerked away from his arm. "Right. Pancakes."

She looked back at the batter and the pan, scared to try again and possibly burn down the house.

Hayden stood to the side with one arm resting on the counter and the other on his hip. "Just say the word, Cadi." He gave a crooked grin.

"Ugh!" Cadence threw up her hands. "Fine! I don't know what I'm doing! I don't know how to cook! What we mixed here is the first time I haven't just added water to something! Are you happy?"

Hayden rubbed his hands together. "I knew it! Now you have to let me teach you."

Cadence put up her hand. "Now, wait a minute. I didn't agree to lessons."

"Oh, yes you did. That was the deal. If you could prove you could cook, I would back off. If not, I got to teach you." He stepped up and sprayed the pan without starting a fire, then quickly grabbed the bowl and a ladle and poured some into the hot surface.

"Too hot," he muttered, turning a knob on the stove. He glanced back. "Well, come on then."

Cadence stepped a little closer. "What exactly am I supposed to do?"

"Come here," he waved her to come in front of him.

"I don't know if that's such a good idea," she whispered, scrunching up her face.

"Cadi, when will you learn that all my ideas are good ideas?" Hayden smirked and tilted his head for her to come.

Heaven save me from arrogant, but adorable men. Slowly, she stepped in front of him and he caged her in. "Notice the bubbles?"

Cadence nodded.

"They'll tell you when a pancake is ready to turn over. We're aiming for a nice golden brown. Okay, looks good. Now, just follow my lead. We're going to flip the pancake." He put the spatula in her hand and then gripped her hand with his. Carefully, he helped her slide under the pancake and with a jerk, they flipped it over.

"Oh my word! We did it!" Cadence grinned over her shoulder and froze. Hayden's face was only inches away. His dark eyes appeared fathomless and Cadence knew she could drown in them if given the chance. *You're gonna regret it if you do this.* Her inner cynic scolded. *He's probably got dozens of women at his beck and call. 'Those at the bottom always want a piece of those at the top.'* Her mind conjured up Ryan's words and the splash of cold water was enough to pull her back to her senses. *Not to mention you still have that date with Oliver coming up.*

With a forced smile, Cadence cleared her throat and stepped out of his arms. Her eyes darted everywhere but at Hayden's obvious disappointment. "So, uh, thanks for the help. I need to run. Got work in the morning, you know."

Hayden shut off the pan, slid the pancake onto a nearby plate and dumped the hot skillet in the sink. "When do you want to have another lesson?"

Cadence gaped. "You're really going to teach me how to cook?"

Hayden scowled. "After all we just went through, you're really asking me that?" He folded his arms and leaned his hips back against the counter. "It's a life skill, Cadi. No one should be eating all that re-hydrated crap. You need real food. I don't know why you never learned while growing up, but we're making up for that now. My schedule is in constant flux, but we can work out times. We can base the meal on the time of day. So how about lunch tomorrow?"

Cadence tucked a chunk of hair behind her ear. "I can probably work that out. Where are we meeting and what should I bring?"

Hayden stroked his chin and stared at the ceiling for a moment. "Meet me in the kitchens and I'll provide the ingredients. Odds are you don't have what we'll need, anyway."

Cadence felt her cheeks heat. "As much as I would like to argue, I think you're right."

Hayden's eyebrows slowly rose, and he grinned. "Excuse me? Did you just agree with me on the first try?"

Cadence held up her hand and started backing toward the door. "Don't let it go to your head. It's already too big."

Hayden put his hand to his chest. "You wound me."

"Ha! That'll be the day." Cadence turned and walked over to the door before pausing. "Shoot." She turned around. "You drove me here so I couldn't leave when I wanted to, didn't you?"

Hayden's grin widened. Standing up he walked over to her and grabbed his keys out of the dish. "Now that you're onto all my tricks, I'll take you home." He held up a finger. "But only if you promise not to stand me up tomorrow."

Cadence rolled her eyes. "I already apologized. I won't do it again, okay?"

Hayden nodded. "I'll hold you to that. Come on."

CHAPTER 10

Hayden found himself grouchier than usual as he went through the breakfast rush the next morning. His evening with Cadence wouldn't leave his mind and he was frustrated that she continued to hold him at arm's length when it was obvious she was just as attracted to him as he was to her.

He whipped his towel over his shoulder and tried to put the subject in the back of his brain, but it wasn't working. After she had stepped back from their almost kiss he had realized just how much he had wanted to kiss her. The disappointment had been palpable. *Why is she so gun shy? Is there something in her past I don't know about?* Hayden thought about Oliver's claim that Cadence came from wealth and it peaked his curiosity. *Maybe she's hiding something...*

CRASH!

Hayden was jolted from his thoughts as a tray full of dishes fell to the ground. Glancing over, he saw two frantic waitresses piling everything on the trays. They were next to the door that led to the dining room and had obviously run into each other going opposite directions.

Hayden stormed over. "What the heck happened?" he growled.

The girls both looked up fearfully and then put their eyes back on the ground.

"Sorry, Chef," one young woman murmured. "It was my fault. I walked through the wrong side."

"No, I should have been looking in front of me, it was my fault, too," the other hurried to say.

Hayden scowled. "Clean this mess up, now! Both of you will report to my office after the shift. Understood?"

They nodded.

"Trevor! Ava! Get over here and help. Then remake those dishes." Hayden's eyes jumped around the room. "Stuart, guard the door so no one else walks into this mess."

"Yes, Chef!"

"On it, Chef!"

"Right away, Chef!"

Hayden grabbed the trays and dumped their contents in the garbage, inwardly moaning at the loss of the food. *Now we're going to be late delivering for the rest of the rush.* "Where's the order ticket?" Hayden shouted at the Tara, one of the waitresses.

She gulped, then pulled it out of her pocket.

Hayden snatched it out of her hands and headed to one of the cooking stations. *Maybe I can get started now so we're not too far behind.*

Despite the rough start to the service, the rest of the breakfast rush ran smoothly. As things settled down, Hayden headed to his office, throwing himself in his chair. He leaned forward onto his elbows and rubbed his temples. "Sometimes I wonder what in the world I was thinking taking on a job like this."

A quiet knock sounded. "Chef?" The two young women were at his door.

"Enter," he said wearily before straightening. He eyed the clock to see how long he had before Cadence arrived. *Only twenty minutes. We'll have to hurry through this.*

The two waitresses came in with their heads bowed. "You wanted to see us, Chef?"

Hayden leaned back and folded his arms. "I understand accidents happen, but most can be avoided if people use their heads. This crash was due to negligence and incompetence," both girls winced as he spoke, but Hayden didn't let it slow him down, "and I won't have it in my kitchen." He stood and walked over in front of the workers. "I teach and train my employees to follow the rules precisely. People expect a certain level of food and experience when they come to my restaurant and I refuse to give them less. If you can't abide by the standards I expect, then you are no longer welcome here," he stated bluntly.

Hayden paused, waiting to see if anyone would speak or defend themselves but the only sound was sniffling. The tears didn't affect him, Hayden had made plenty of other employees cry and he wasn't about to worry about one more.

"What do you have to say for yourselves? Rebecca? Tara?"

When he called them by name, they both shot their heads up. Tara's eyes were red and wet, while Rebecca's face was hard. *A fighter. Good. She'll do better here.*

He folded his arms and stared them down.

Tara was the first to break. "I'm so sorry, Chef, but please don't fire me. I need this job. I promise to do better. I went through the wrong door, but I won't do it again."

Hayden raised an eyebrow but didn't speak. His eyes shifted to Rebecca.

"I apologize, Chef. It won't happen again," she said through clenched teeth.

Hayden narrowed his eyes. *Pushing the line, little girl,* he thought. "Fine," he said curtly. "But if anything even close to this ever happens again, you'll both be gone. Is that understood?"

"Yes, Chef. Thank you, Chef," Tara stammered out.

Rebecca nodded but her rigid jaw only relaxed slightly.

"Tara, you may go. Rebecca, I'd like to talk to you privately." Hayden lifted his chin toward the door.

Tara tumbled over a few more 'thank you's' before she disappeared through his office door. Hayden walked backward until he sat down in his chair. Tilting his head, he studied the waitress in front of him. "You've got spirit, Rebecca, but that anger is going to get you in trouble. You were involved in a crash that put my kitchen and staff behind this morning, not to mention wasted multiple plates of food and cost me money in dishes. Why do you have the right to be angry?"

Rebecca's face had hardened again, but this time tears filled her eyes and her fists clenched. She didn't answer for several moments, but Hayden was willing to wait her out.

"I'm willing to wait all night, Rebecca."

She worked her jaw for a moment before her shoulders slumped and her chin fell to her chest. "I thought you were going to fire us."

"Could you have blamed me if I did?"

She shrugged. "I know I took some blame for the accident but she shouldn't have been going through the wrong door. I need this job and the thought of losing it because of someone else's actions had me on edge. I'm sorry, Chef."

Hayden nodded. "Why do you need this job so badly?"

Rebecca's head shot up and suspicion clouded her features. "Why do you care?"

"I know what desperation looks like. I've been there."

She narrowed her eyes and studied him. She pinched her lips into a tight line then let out a long breath. "I have a little boy at home. If I'm not working, he's not eating."

"I see," Hayden said quietly. "What about you? Are you able to feed yourself as well? Where's the boy father?"

Her lower lip trembled and she bit it to stop the shake. "He left when I got pregnant. And I manage to eat enough."

"Family?"

"No," she said bluntly. "And it's really none of your business."

"Fair enough," Hayden answered. Leaning forward, he looked her in the eye. "Did you know that we have extra food left over every night after our dinner rush?"

"No..." she said warily.

Hayden nodded. "It's pretty wasteful, but that's the business. I donate what I can, but not everything can be sent to a food bank. If people such as yourself were to load up a container and take it home, it would go a long way in helping keep our landfills clean."

The tears that had been threatening for the last few minutes finally spilled down her cheeks. "I don't do charity."

Hayden snorted. "This isn't charity. It's good business sense. Food is meant to be eaten, not thrown away. Not to mention my food is too good to go to waste."

The muscles in her body finally relaxed a little, and the tears subsided. "Do you really mean that? You're not just making this up?"

"Do I have any sort of reputation as a nice guy?" Hayden scoffed. "Look, everyone has some kind of sob story. I can't give raises based on people's home lives or I'd run myself out of business. But we throw plenty of food away in the evenings and if you took some home for you and your kid, then that's just that much less my other workers have to haul outside."

Rebecca clenched her hands against her middle. "Yes, Chef. Thank you, Chef."

Hayden nodded. "You're dismissed."

With a watery smile, she darted out the door.

Hayden ran his hands through his hair and blew a loud breath out between his lips. "Now if only my evening with Cadence had gone as well." He paused. "Maybe some food would go a long way in softening her attitude as well."

CADENCE FOUND HERSELF unable to concentrate all morning. She had gotten home from her 'cooking lesson' with Hayden and had been so wired, she'd barely slept. And now here she was, more jittery than a kid on caffeine.

With a groan, she buried her face in her hands. "Ugh. How am I going to do this? Every time I get close to him I want to kiss him. This is so ridiculous." She shook her head. "I'm too old to be acting like a teenager, but sheesh, every time he gets close or does something silly, I'm falling further."

Ryan. Remember Ryan. "And Oliver!" she yelled into her empty office. "Man." She rubbed her throbbing forehead. "I wish I hadn't agreed to that second date. It was already clear that nothing was going to happen between us. Stupid pride."

Her phone buzzed, drawing her attention away from her moanings. With a sigh she answered. "Hey, Mom."

"When are you coming home?"

"Nice to talk to you, too. I'm good, thank you for asking." Cadence sent a prayer heavenward for patience.

"Enough. Cadence, we've been lenient enough. Ryan says you won't take his calls, and that's just ridiculous. You need to stop being a baby, quit your job and come home where you belong."

Cadence clenched her fist and knocked herself on the forehead. "Mom, do you even hear yourself? Leaving a man who was cheating on me is not being a baby. You may be all right with that kind of life, but I'm not! I want a man who wants me and will be loyal to only me."

Her mother scoffed.

"In fact, most of the population wants that, Mom. It's not too much to ask. As for the other things, I like my job. I've made friends here and I refuse to walk out and leave them in a lurch over something as dumb as money."

"Money is what has paid for your whole lifestyle, dear daughter. Those nice clothes? Came from money. That hair? Money. Your fancy education? Money. But go on, please keep telling me how much you loathe the very thing that makes the world go round."

"I didn't say I loathed money. I simply said it wasn't the most important thing. Stop twisting my words." Cadence could feel her temper rising and she knew she was about to lose it.

"I give up," Arianna said, her voice away from the speaker. "You talk some sense into her." There was a shuffling and then quiet.

"Hello?" Cadence asked with a frown.

"Hello, Cadi-bear," her father said.

Cadence sighed. "Hi, Dad"

"You made your mother mad."

"Yeah. I got that."

"So, any chance that you'll come home? One of these days the media is going to find out my daughter is working rather than just visiting relatives. Do you know what they're going to say about me? And what about your engagement to Ryan? All of California is waiting to hear wedding plans and you're not here."

"Dad!" Cadence moaned. "I'm not sure how many times I have to say this, but my engagement to Ryan is over. Got it? OVER! I'm not coming back. Your political aspirations will just have to do without me. And nobody is going to care if I'm working rather than living off your dime. In fact, I'll bet most of them will think it's about time an Everwood woman did something other than hang off a man's arm."

"Cadence, you push too far," her father growled. "Politics is a family affair and you know that it will look better if you're here with us rather than gone during the whole election. How will it look if we have to suddenly tell people you and Ryan aren't together any more? He plans to run in the next couple of years. You're ruining his chances if you walk away."

"Dad." Cadence's jaw was clenched, and it hurt to speak. "I don't know how to make this any clearer than I have. I broke up with Ryan almost a year ago. It isn't even close to being sudden. And I'm not the one ruining his career, he did by being a cheater and a scumbag."

"Cadi-bear-"

"Stop calling me that. I'm not five any more. Now," she straightened in her seat and smoothed her shirt down, "if you and Mom continue to push me, I will not only cut all ties, but I'll go to the media myself. I mean it. I've made my choice and I'm not going back on it. Either get on board with that, or we're done."

Her father sighed. "I'll give you some time to think about it," he said gruffly. "Have a good day, I've got to go speak to your mother."

"You do that." Cadence hung up. She clenched her phone for a moment, fighting the urge to throw it across the room. "Unbelievable." She laughed harshly. "How can someone be in such complete denial? Has he never been told 'no' before?"

Her stomach growled, and she quickly covered it with a hand. Glancing at the clock, she realized it was time for her to head to the kitchen. "From one rich guy to another." Cadence gave a sarcastic laugh and shook her head. "This is exactly why I want nothing to do with men like that." *Now if I could just get my heart to remember.*

"At least we're meeting at the restaurant," she muttered as she walked down the hallway. "That'll keep him on his best behavior."

Once at the kitchen, she carefully slipped through the back door. The space was quieter than usual. Only a few workers sat at workstations, chopping or prepping food items. *Dang it. I thought there would be more people around.*

Cadence chewed the inside of her cheek in indecision. "No, I told him I would come. It's not okay for me to back out of that," she muttered to herself.

When she didn't see Hayden right away, she walked over to one of the workers. "Excuse me, could you tell me were Hay- I mean Chef Truman is?"

"He's in his office," the young man said, pointing his knife toward the back corner.

"Got it. Thanks," Cadence smiled and walked away. Just as she approached the office, a young woman with a tear-streaked face came out. "Are you okay?" Cadence hurried to her side. "Hayden!" Cadence looked in the door and glared at him. "What have you done this time? You can't just go around yelling at people all the time!"

Hayden scowled. "I didn't yell!"

"If I have to-" Cadence started, but the woman in front of her grabbed her arm.

"No, no, no. It's okay. There's been a misunderstanding." She gave Cadence a reassuring smile. "We were just having a chat. It's okay."

Cadence narrowed her eyes. *What are they hiding?*

"Really. It's fine. Everything's fine." The waitress looked back at Hayden. "Thank you, Chef." With another smile at Cadence, the young woman turned and walked out.

Cadence watched her go. *Maybe I've been reading Hayden wrong. Maybe he isn't interested in me.* Jealousy slammed into Cadence and it nearly took her breath away. *Stop it!* she screamed at herself. *He's not yours. He can be with whoever he wants. It's not like we're dating. I mean, I still have a dinner date with Oliver on Friday.*

She turned to look at Hayden, who was watching her intently. "Are you still wanting to make lunch?"

"Why wouldn't we?"

"Well," Cadence waved an arm in the direction the other woman left, "won't your girlfriend be upset at us spending time together?"

Hayden eyes lit up, and he smiled. "Cadi Everwood. Are you jealous?"

Her eyes widened. "What? No. Absolutely not. It just- well it seemed that-" She shook her head. "It doesn't matter."

Hayden stepped up close, bringing his fresh bread scent that always made Cadence's mouth water. "We're not dating. We had business to take care of and she got emotional. She's just a waitress in my restaurant. Nothing more."

Cadence tried to look nonchalant. "It doesn't matter to me who you talk to. I'm not your keeper."

"What if I want you to be?"

Fear mixed with desire swam through her. *What is he saying? Is he just flirting? Does he say that to all the girls?* "Well, then I guess it's a good thing it's not up to just you, huh?" *Why is my voice all breathy? Get it together, Everwood!*

"We'll see," he said enigmatically. With a smirk, he stepped back and Cadence felt like she could breathe again.

Her stomach rumbled and Hayden laughed. "Come on. Let's go fix some food."

"Food. Sounds good." She followed quietly behind Hayden as he led her to a counter.

"I thought we would do something really simple, since it's lunch."

"'Kay."

"I'm going to show you how to make a sandwich," Hayden stated as he walked away to gather ingredients.

Cadence stood frozen. "A sandwich? Really?"

He paused. "Yeah. What's the problem?"

Cadence huffed and crossed her arms. "I thought you were teaching me how to cook. Making a sandwich doesn't involve cooking. Even I can throw some meat onto a piece of bread with mayo."

Hayden made a gagging noise. "And that is exactly why I'm going to teach you what to do. You can do much better than that."

Her stomach rumbled again. "Whatever. I guess as long as I get to eat it's no big deal."

"Did you eat breakfast?" He set some rolls and cheese on the counter.

"Nah, didn't get around to it." Cadence began reading the labels of what he was setting down.

"Weren't you ever taught that breakfast is the most important meal of the day?"

"Sure. What kid wasn't taught that in school?"

"Obviously you, either that or you were a poor student."

Cadence snapped to look at him and give him a piece of her mind, but the grin on his face stopped the words on the tip of her lips. *He's playing with me. Huh. Maybe he's not quite as grumpy as he pretends to be.* "Maybe you should just give up on teaching me, then. Maybe I'm hopeless."

He shrugged. "Or maybe you just needed the right teacher." His eyes smoldered and suddenly Cadence wasn't sure they were still talking about sandwiches.

Oh my word. Who turned up the heater? She resisted the urge to fan her face, instead choosing to keep her focus on the ingredients they had gathered. "Okay, Yoda. Teach me sandwich magic."

His lips quirked into a half grin. "Patience, Padiwan. These things take time."

Cadence laughed.

"The thing to remember is that it's all about the bread and spread."

Fifteen minutes later they were sitting at a table eating.

"Oh my gosh, this is sooo good!" she said around a mouthful of half-chewed food.

Hayden chuckled and handed her a napkin.

Cadence wiped the crumbs from her lips and swallowed. "Thanks." She took a drink of her soda. "I mean I've eaten a lot of good food in my life, but I had no idea a sandwich could be this amazing. You were totally right. The bread makes a huge difference. Did you make this?"

Hayden nodded.

"No wonder you always smell so good," she mumbled before taking another bite. When she straightened, Hayden was frowning.

"If you grew up eating good food, how come you don't know how to cook? I assumed you didn't learn because your mother didn't know how."

Ah, man. Me and my big mouth. "Oh, I uh, I just meant that I've eaten at a lot of good restaurants. California is full of them, you know."

"And you could afford to eat out all the time?"

Cadence shrugged. "Enough."

He grunted and chewed his bite.

"So, what made you decide to become a chef?"

Hayden's shoulders shook a little.

"What's so funny?" Cadence took another bite.

"If I had a nickel for every time someone asked me that question…"

Cadence rolled her eyes. "Well, I've never asked, and I would like to know."

Hayden cleared his throat and tapped his chest with his fist. "Once upon a time, there was a little boy who loved food. He used to spend all his free time in the kitchen with his mother, learning how to make everything his heart desired. In fact, he loved it so much that he was bigger than all the other kids."

Cadence's head jerked toward him.

"Nobody liked the kid, and he got made fun of all the time. However, instead of taking what they were dishing out, this kid got angry. He fought back at the bullies and continued his love affair with fine ingredients. One day the middle school coach talked him into playing football because he had more bulk than anyone else and he learned to channel his aggressive nature into winning. Not to mention it helped turn all that bulk into muscles rather than jelly."

Cadence's hands, still holding her sandwich, fell into her lap. *Oh my word. How awful!*

"So, the boy became a winner, but he never lost his love for food, so when he got out of high school, he put the two of them together and became a top chef."

Cadence's jaw fell as he picked up his sandwich and took a bite. "I don't even know what to say."

Hayden's eyes darted around the room then at her. "What's to say?"

"It's so sad. Not to mention I would have never guessed that you were bullied as a kid."

"Aren't we all bullied?"

Not when you're considered California royalty. Cadence knew people catered to her family. They probably talked behind her back, in fact, she was sure they had. The people in the elite circles were often catty and jealous. But no one had ever said anything to her face, and she wasn't sure what she would have done if they had. "I suppose…" she hedged. "You must have had an amazing mom. How did she handle all this?"

Hayden's lips tilted down. "Mom, uh, well mom was the perfect little homemaker. Her favorite thing to do was take bread and cookies to the neighbors. I think she thought she could individually get rid of crime, if she could simply bake enough."

An ache began in Cadence's chest. *What would that have been like?*

"But don't get me wrong, she raised five kids, so that woman knew how to handle a fight." He chuckled, but kept his eye on his sandwich.

"Have your parents been to see the resort yet? Is she excited about you being a chef?"

He cleared his throat. "Nope. I was just getting ready to graduate when they were killed."

Cadence gasped. "What?"

"Laken and Teagan, my sisters-" he raised an eyebrow asking if she remembered who they were and Cadence nodded, "-had just headed off to college. Mom and Dad were leaving on their very first 'empty nester' vacation and were struck by a drunk driver."

"Oh my goodness," Cadence's eyes filled up with tears. "No wonder you-" She shook her head. "Never mind. I'm so sorry for your loss."

"We've managed." He stuffed a bite in his mouth.

"You know, it's okay to admit you have feelings." Cadence pinched her lips together, frustrated at his brush off.

"What do you want me to say? It was rough? Yeah, it was. My parents were all that is good in this world. Married for thirty years, helped their neighbors, active in their church. I almost let go of culinary school when my mom was taken. But I didn't. I knew she'd be so mad at me if I let my life go to waste. So, I finished. I finished first in my class and I went on to be one of the youngest head chefs ever hired in New York." He took a long sip of his soda. "And now, I run a restaurant of my own. And just like before, I demand perfection. I'm not a nice guy, Cadi, I mean my mama taught me manners and stuff, but I've only gotten where I am because I push. I don't give up. Life throws horrible things at us sometimes. We can either cower like scared little babies or we can stand up and fight back."

Cadence sat frozen, listening to his little rampage. *I had no idea. First bullied, then losing his parents. No wonder he's harsh.* When she realized her heart was starting to soften even further toward the attractive man in front of her, she knew it was time to get going. *If I don't leave, I'm going to admit I'm falling for him or something else equally as terrible.* "I need to finish so I can get back to work." Cadence shoved an unladylike bite into her mouth.

"When are we having your next lesson?" Hayden wiped his mouth, completely nonplussed at the change in topic.

Cadence pursed her lips. "I don't know. My schedule is more open than yours. What works for you?"

"I can slip away for a few hours tomorrow afternoon if you want to go grocery shopping."

Cadence wrinkled her nose. "Grocery shopping? What does that have to do with anything?"

He raised an eyebrow. "Are you seriously asking me that question? How can you cook if you don't have the right food? You don't even have flour in your little postage stamp house."

"Hey!" She leaned over and bumped shoulders with him. "That postage stamp came with the job and I'm grateful for it."

Hayden put his hands in the air. "Whatever tickles your fancy. At least I don't have to worry about you being after my money if you're happy in that dumpy little place."

Cadence froze. "I'm not... I would never... we're not..." Quickly she stood from where they were sitting. "I gotta run. Thank you for lunch."

"Cadence." Hayden's stern voice stopped her mid flight. He walked over and stood in front of her. Reaching out he gently tugged on her chin until she looked him in the eye. "I'll text you about tomorrow," he said quietly.

"Why are you bothering with all this? Am I just another challenge?" *Please say no. Wait. No. Say yes. I mean... oh my word, I'm in such trouble.*

Slowly, he shook his head. "I always get what I want."

Cadence's heart sank. *Well, what did you expect? For him to admit his undying love for you? You aren't even dating, Cadence.* Her mind flittered back to why she had left home in the first place and then how hard it had been ever since. "There's always a first time," she said hoarsely before stepping around him and darting through the door.

CHAPTER 11

When Cadence arrived at her office the next morning, it took her a few minutes to realize there was something on her desk. She'd put her briefcase down, hung her jacket up and woke up her computer before reaching over to grab some papers she had left on the side of her desk.

"Ouch," she said when her hand ran into a metal item. Looking over, she gasped. A metal cloche sat covering a plate. She eyed the dish. Tentatively, she reached out and lifted the lid. Fragrant steam gushed into the air. "Mmm... oh my word." She closed her eyes and breathed in the savory smell.

Opening her eyes, she reached out and picked up the plate, putting it in front of her. A ramekin of quiche, fresh fruit and three of Hayden's homemade sausage links stared up at her. *Why did Hayden send this?* She wasn't sure how things were between them after the way she left yesterday. With every touch and sweet gesture, she found her defenses against him melting. And especially after hearing about his family and childhood, the nurturing side of her just wanted to hug him and make it all better. *How do I keep my distance after all this?*

After saying a quick prayer of thanks, she dug in, moaning as the quiche melted on her tongue. *Oh my gosh, that man can cook.* When she had finished, she set the plate aside, and noticed an envelope sitting under the plate.

Grabbing it, she opened the note.

Grocery store. Two. Don't be late.

She snorted. "If his ego gets any bigger, he won't fit in the castle," she said through a laugh, then paused. "Oh my word, I'm in such trouble. I'm not even put off by his arrogance anymore." She sighed and rubbed her hands down the front of her face. "What am I gonna do?" She paused. "Do I want to do anything?" She felt the first stirrings of panic begin to work their way through her system. "How do I know he's not just like Ryan? They're both wealthy, good looking and full of themselves. Can Hayden really be that different? I mean, he is different, he wasn't raised the same as Ryan, but still. How do I know Hayden isn't just playing me as well?" She huffed. "Stop it, Cadence. He hasn't asked you to date him or anything. You're going to the grocery store for crying out loud. There is absolutely nothing romantic about it." Grabbing a pencil and paper she decided to write him back.

Dear Hayden,

Thank you for breakfast. I look forward to learning the inner workings of the mysterious grocery store. Us non-food people have been waiting years for someone to unlock the mysteries behind this industry. I have no doubt your knowledge will be most invaluable.

Cadence

She reread the note several times, then nodded and grinned. *We might not be dating, but flirting with someone just as sarcastic as myself is certainly fun.*

After finding an employee to run the dishes and note back to Hayden, she pushed the incident to the back of her mind and went to work.

Several hours went by and she was surprised when she finally looked up from her computer to realize it was lunch time. With a sigh, she shut down the document she had been working on, grabbed an apple and meal replacement bar out of her briefcase and headed over to lounge on her couch.

Taking a bite, Cadence sighed, kicked off her heels and put her feet on the coffee table. *Finally, a moment to relax.* Moments later, she jumped when someone knocked. "What now?" she groaned. Setting her food down, she went to open the door.

"Hi, Ms. Everwood. Mr. Truman asked me to bring this to you." The young woman held a tray with another plate and cloche on it.

Cadence blinked several times. "I-" Cadence found herself at a loss for words. *What is Hayden doing?* She cleared her throat. "Thank you," she told the worker. Cadence scooted back and opened the door wider. "You can set it right over there."

Once the young lady had set it down, she stood awkwardly shifting her weight from side to side.

"Is there something you need?" Cadence asked walking toward the desk.

The girl tugged on her hair. "The staff and me, we were just wondering if you two were, you know, dating?"

Cadence panicked. "What two? Me and Hayden? Absolutely, not."

The girl's shoulders fell. "Oh."

"You were hoping we were, I mean you were really hoping we were together?" Cadence asked in shock.

"Well, yeah. Chef Truman never goes on dates. So, we were excited to see him paying attention to you." The young woman frowned.

"Why you would care about his relationships? Don't you all hate him?" Cadence pinched her lips between her teeth as soon as the words were out of her mouth. *That wasn't a nice thing to ask. I shouldn't have said anything.*

The worker smiled. "Seems like we would, huh? He's pretty demanding. But honestly, in the culinary world, he's not that much worse than most head chefs. And he's got the experience and credentials behind him to ask for what he does." She shrugged. "He's tough. And I would never describe him as my friend or anything, but if you can hack it in his kitchen, you can hack it anywhere. I guess most of us wear it like a badge of honor."

"Huh," Cadence was at a loss. "So you actually... like him?"

"Maybe respect is a better word. None of us get close enough to him to really like him. But we do care about him and believe it or not, he cares about us. He just doesn't let other people know it." She glanced at the door then leaned in and dropped her voice. "He'd never admit to it, but Chef Truman paid the medical bill when Travis nearly took his finger off. Travis is saving money for college and he was going to have to make payments for the stitches, but a couple of weeks later, he got a phone call that everything had been paid for by an anonymous source."

"How do you know it was Hayden? I mean Chef Truman?"

"Who else has money to splash around like that?" The girl scrunched up her face. "Anyway, most of us think you two would make a great couple. You're always so nice you'd probably soften him up a bit. Not to mention you guys would have the world's most beautiful babies." She giggled.

Cadence felt the blush rise rapidly up through her neck and into her cheeks. "Uh, gotcha. Thanks. I appreciate you bringing the tray."

Still smiling, the worker walked back to the door and grabbed the knob. "No prob," she said before slipping through and closing the door.

Cadence walked slowly to her desk and plopped down in the seat. Hesitantly, she lifted the lid off the plate. "Breakfast, now lunch." She rubbed her forehead. "What is he doing? And now I find out that his workers actually like him. The world has gone haywire, and he's ruining my opinion of his jerkiness."

Glancing around the tray, Cadence spotted the note. She opened and read it. *Aaand there he is.*

It's about time we established who was in charge.

Shaking her head with a mixture of annoyance and fondness, she dug into the delicious meal.

Later that afternoon, Cadence pushed her shopping cart through the small lanes of the grocery store. With every squeak of the front wheel, she told herself she should just go home. "The more time you spend with him, the harder it is to stay in the friend zone," she grumbled. Cadence gave a small smile when the woman in front of her turned. "Sorry. Just talking to myself."

"It's all right, dear, we all do that from time to time. Excuse me for blocking the aisle, I'll only be a minute." The elderly woman smiled and went back to her debate over the canned soups in front of her.

"No worries," Cadence said with a sigh. "Can I help you with anything?"

"Oh, no." The lady chuckled. "I'm just not sure what I'm in the mood for."

Cadence smiled and nodded. She glanced around at the shelves as she waited for the other patron to finish up. *Where is Hayden? He's late. Ha! He'd probably fire a worker who showed up late. Maybe I should fire him as my teacher.*

Cadence started walking again, the other woman having finally dumped a few cans in her cart and moved on. Cadence tucked her own cart to the side to avoid blocking the aisle and browsed the cans of soup herself. Grabbing one, she read the directions on the back. "Surely, these can't be too hard to make, right?" She muttered.

"You aren't seriously thinking about buying that, are you?"

Cadence closed her eyes and worked to hold her smile in check. *I'm in so much trouble.* She turned and leaned one elbow on the cart. "Hello, Hayden. Fancy meeting you here."

Hayden raised an eyebrow. "Yeah. Isn't it quite the coincidence?" He stepped closer to her. Cadence stood her ground and did her best to ignore the quickening of her pulse and breathing. "Today has been a bit rough, so to find you here seems... fortuitous."

Cadence snorted. "Fortuitous? Who speaks like that?"

Hayden smirked. "Who says 'fancy meeting you here'?"

"Well, obviously I did."

"And obviously, I used fortuitous."

Cadence felt her lips twitch, but she continued to hold in her smile. *Don't do it, Cadence. It will only encourage him.*

"Oh, don't hold it back. I'm sure it does wonders for you."

Cadence frowned. "What?"

Hayden leaned down close. "Your smile. I've learned firsthand that you're a softy under that prickly exterior, so I'm pretty sure a smile won't crack your face. Let it loose."

Cadence put her hands on his chest and shoved him backward a couple of steps. "With words such as that, it's a wonder you don't have women beating down your door." She grabbed her cart and left him behind.

The infuriating man caught up with her. "What have you got in here?" He pulled on her cart until she stopped.

"Hayden, stop that!" She took the box of pasta out of his hands and dropped it back in.

"How can you eat that stuff? It tastes like cardboard." He crossed his arms and smiled. "This is why I'm teaching you to cook, so you don't have to eat garbage."

Cadence rolled her eyes. "Maybe so, but while I'm still learning, I'm still going to have to feed myself. You can't send me trays forever." Cadence paused. "Speaking of which, that was really nice of you. Thank you."

Hayden grinned. "You sound surprised. I've been trying to tell you I'm a good guy."

"Actually, I think you told me just the opposite."

He shook his head. "No, I said I'm not a nice guy. But I am a *good* guy. There's a difference."

"Whatever. Are we shopping or what?"

"Yep. Come on." He grabbed the front of her cart and started pulling her along. His eyes were on the shelves and after a minute he grabbed a few bags and put them in her cart.

"What is that?" She grabbed one of the items he had put in. "Couscous? That sounds hard."

Hayden grinned. "That's why you have me."

Cadence sighed. "Why do I feel like I'm digging myself into a hole?"

He put a hand to his chest. "Ouch! That stung."

Cadence sent her eyes heavenward, pleading for help. "I'm sure you'll survive." She started to push the cart and almost ran into another customer. "Oh! Sorry," she cried.

The man glared at her before continuing on his way.

When Cadence started walking again, she glanced over her shoulder to find Hayden holding in his snicker with a fist over his mouth. "Knock it off," she growled.

"I didn't realize I was going to have to teach you grocery store etiquette as well," he laughed as he caught back up to her.

Cadence's cheeks felt like they were hot enough to start a fire. "You are the most exasperating man ever."

Hayden wrapped an arm around her waist and pulled her back against his chest. Every nerve ending in Cadence's body went on alert.

"What are you doing?" she hissed over her shoulder.

"I only tease those I like, so you should take it as a compliment."

Cadence closed her eyes for a moment. It felt so right to be tucked up against him and she could never get enough of the smell that followed Hayden everywhere he went. *What is it about fresh baked carbs that is so appealing?* When Hayden's chuckle rumbled against her back, her eyes shot open and she darted out of his arms.

She cleared her throat. "If incessant teasing is for those you like, I pity the people you dislike."

"Me too," Hayden whispered in her ear before darting to the front of the cart again.

"Get a room," a teenage boy muttered as he slinked past them, carrying a small basket.

"Thanks, buddy!" Hayden called out.

Cadence closed her eyes and did her best to push down the curse words trying to work their way out of her mouth. "Hayden," she said with a harsh sigh.

"You need to let your hair down and learn to live a little. Quit worrying about what other people think."

"Why is it when I'm around you, I don't know whether to laugh or to cry?"

Hayden chuckled as he tossed more stuff in the cart. "I guess that's an improvement. Not too long ago you only wanted to yell."

That was before you showed me you could actually be nice. It was easier to resist when you were just an attractive jerk. Now you're a sweet, attractive jerk. Aargh. Why is everything so hard?

HAYDEN DID HIS BEST to hold back his laugh at her reactions, but she was just so attractive when she got worked up. Her cheeks flushed and her eyes flashed. He was having a hard time not kissing those perfect lips, which at this moment were pursed into the most delectable pout. *Not yet, buddy. Keep it together.*

"Let's head to the produce and grab some fresh veggies and I'll teach you how to make a stir fry," he said over his shoulder. He grinned when she rolled her eyes at him, but turned the corner anyway.

After picking up several different kinds of peppers and other things, he walked them up to the check-out stand. Together they loaded the food onto the conveyor belt. When Cadence tried to step up to pay, Hayden held out his arm. "Hey, hold up. I got this."

"Excuse me?" Cadence huffed and cocked her hip. "These are my groceries. I am perfectly capable of paying for my own food."

"I'm sure you are, but I had you get things you wouldn't normally have bought and so I'll take care of the bill." He winked and leaned in. "Don't worry, I'm good for it."

Cadence rolled her eyes and shook her head. "No thanks, rich boy. I'd rather pay my own way."

Hayden backed up with his hands up. "Fine, have it your way." He walked around her to bag the groceries.

"Well hello, Mr. Truman," the young cashier said with a smile.

"Stacy." He nodded. "How's your day going?" This was the closest grocery store to the resort, so Hayden or one of his employees could be found here often. As such, he knew a fair number of the store workers well.

"Better now that you're here," she giggled.

Hayden groaned inwardly. In an attempt to not encourage her further, he nodded, but didn't speak again. He glanced at Cadence in his periphery and noticed she was stoic. *Is that good or bad? Does she care that the cashier is flirting?* He wanted to growl and shake her shoulders to get answers out of her. He felt pretty sure she was attracted to him, judging from the way she reacted to his presence. But something was holding her back. Every time he got too close, she ran like a scared rabbit. He'd been trying to earn her trust, but he was getting impatient. *Meeting her in the restaurant and at grocery stores doesn't give me much room to make a move. I'm going to have to do something else soon.*

After walking her to her car, he helped load the bags. "You're awfully quiet. What's got you tied up like a trussed pig?"

"You have the most lovely metaphors," she grumbled.

"Answer the question, Cadi," Hayden said in an exasperated tone.

Her bright blue eyes pierced through him. "Fine. Back there at the checkout stand, I was just reminded of why I avoid men like you."

Hayden jerked back. "Men like me? What exactly does that mean?"

"I mean rich, handsome men who think they can string girls along. Who think their wealth and power allows them special privileges and that they are the exception to every rule."

"You got all that from my interaction with Stacy?" Hayden could feel his temper brewing, but he held it back for the time being. Cadence had been holding something against him since they met and he was determined to get it out of her.

"Yes," she said through clenched teeth.

"So I'm not allowed to say hello to anyone? That sounds very much against those good manners you always preach about." Hayden crossed his arms and leaned his hip against the car.

Cadence clenched her fists and growled before throwing her hands out and deflating. "I'm sorry. That was completely uncalled for. I'm being catty and I have no right to be." She rubbed her forehead. "Can we just forget I said anything?"

Hayden narrowed his eyes for a moment. *Why can't she just admit she's jealous? Or that she has feelings for me? That's what I want, isn't it? I mean, yeah, this all started as a challenge, but is that how I still feel?* Multiple emotions swam through Hayden, but the most prominent was confusion. *I've got to figure this out myself before I can ask the same of her.*

"Yeah. That's fine. We should probably both go cool off."

Cadence's shoulders fell in relief. "Thank you."

"Come by my house tomorrow around eight and we'll cook up dinner. Bring the stuff I had you buy."

Cadence nodded. "Sounds good. Thanks." Stepping around him, she got in her car and waited until he was out of the way to pull out and drive back toward the resort.

Hayden watched her go, feeling slightly lost. *What is going on with me? I can't get her out of my head and the harder she fights, the more I want her. But why do I want her? I guess that's the million dollar question...*

CHAPTER 12

T he next night, Cadence knocked on Hayden's door. Her nerves were in knots and it took all her concentration to keep the grocery bags she held from shaking. She had had a revelation at the grocery store the afternoon before and it was tearing her apart.

When that clerk had flirted with Hayden, Cadence had been livid. *Who knew the green-eyed monster was so powerful?* Even that slight interaction, which Hayden had not pursued, was enough to send Cadence over the edge.

She tapped her foot as she waited for him to answer the door. *I'm falling for this guy. A guy who is everything I swore I didn't want. And I'm falling for him. But now what? He hasn't tried to kiss me again since that first time. Maybe he doesn't feel the same way? Maybe I really am just a challenge to him.*

"Sorry. I was on the other side of the cabin. Come on in." Hayden stepped back to let her in.

Cadence snorted. "I don't think this qualifies as a cabin."

"It's made of logs. It's totally a cabin." Hayden reached down to the bags she was carrying. "Let me get those."

"Huh. I guess chivalry isn't dead after all."

"It's never been dead. It's just been turned down." Hayden smirked.

"I'm not even going there. We argue enough as it is."

"Can it really count as arguing when we're both enjoying ourselves?" He set the bags down on the kitchen counter.

Cadence stepped up and started helping unload the groceries. "How do you know I enjoy it? Maybe I hate the fact that we argue all the time."

Hayden leaned down close to her ear. "Oh, I know you love it because you keep coming back for more."

A tremor ran down her spine and Cadence gasped quietly. She was so torn. *Do I give in and take the risk he's just like Ryan? Or keep holding back and stay lonely?*

"Ready to make some stir-fry?" Hayden swept up a bunch of the ingredients and carried them over to his butcher block.

No! I want to go back to the little moment we just had. She sighed. *Too late.* "Yep. Waiting this late to eat makes me really hungry."

Hayden laughed lightly. "Chefs eat at all hours. It's pretty rare to run a normal schedule."

Cadence nodded. "I can see how that would be true."

"Chop these, would you?"

"Uh," Cadence picked up the pepper he had pushed her way. "Knife?"

He nodded toward a block on the counter.

Holy cow. He doesn't have to worry about home invaders. Cadence eyed the dozens of sharp objects, debating which one to take. Finally, she settled on a small one. *This way I won't cut myself.*

"Nope. That's a fillet knife. Not what you're looking for."

"Oh." She looked at the knife, then put it back. "So what am I looking for?"

"Use the chef's knife, the San Moritz." Hayden reached above his head to grab a large skillet.

Cadence huffed. "You know full well I don't know what that is."

After setting the pan down he walked up behind her. "This is a chef's knife." He grabbed a large, long knife off the block. "It's used for chopping and dicing. We want you to put the pepper into long, thin, strips, so it's the best guy for the job."

"Okay," she said in a soft voice with her eyes closed. *Oooh, I've got it bad.*

"Everything okay?" Hayden leaned in close to her ear.

It would be if you kissed me. "Uh... Yes... maybe..."

He chuckled and leaned his arms around her, holding onto the counter top. "Which is it, Ms. Cadi?" Hayden ran his nose around her ear.

Cadence's heart felt like it might burst out of her chest. *Ryan never made me feel like this. Hayden's got to be different. Right? He's got to be.*

"Are you going to answer me?" His hands came up and held onto her upper arms and he slowly turned her until they faced each other.

Cadence could tell her eyes were wide and her cheeks flushed. Her hands automatically came up between them, landing on his chest.

Hayden's eyes roamed her face, studying, caressing. He ran the back of his finger down her cheek. "What is this, Cadi? Do you feel it too?" His voice was hoarse and the tenderness in it hit Cadence straight in her heart.

"Yes! Wait. No. Ugh! I don't know!" Cadence stepped out of his arms and began to pace. "I can't think straight around you. I get all messed up inside and you make me feel things I've never felt before. You are exactly the type of guy I came out here to avoid!" She paused and waved an arm in his direction. "How am I supposed to avoid you when you act all nice and stuff. When you were just the good-looking jerk in the kitchen it wasn't as hard, but now..." She pushed her fingers into her hair. "Now you're being sweet. You're sending me food. You say hi to other women without flirting with them even though they try to flirt with you. I mean, ha!" she laughed derisively. "Even your kitchen workers like you. The very ones you yell at all the time! You're not supposed to be like that! I mean, what exactly am I supposed to do with that?"

Hayden crossed his arms and leaned back against the countertop, watching her move. "What do you want to do with it?"

"Oh, don't throw this all back on me, Buddy," She wagged a finger at him. "What do you want to do with it?" She stopped and put her hands on her hips. "You kiss me senseless and then never do it again. What's a woman supposed to think?"

Hayden rolled his eyes. "That if he tried again he'd get slapped? You haven't exactly been the most welcoming person, Cadi."

He's right. He's so right. You've held him off for a long time. "You're right." Her shoulders drooped. "You're right." She put her hands on her head and walked a little more. "I've been... I've been afraid."

"Of what?" Hayden finally asked when she didn't say more.

How much do I tell him? Is it really that big of a deal if he knows about my family? She stood next to the counter and drew designs on the granite. "Of getting hurt, I guess. Of feeling like leftovers. The last guy I was with was like you. He had money, looks, status, and he also thought that if he fooled around on the side, it didn't matter. That I should just be content with the fact that he always kept me around."

"Are you kidding me? Who thinks like that?" Hayden growled.

Cadence looked up at him from beneath her eyelashes. "Men with wealth and power. He's not the only one I know who thinks that's okay."

"Well, then you've been hanging around the wrong men." He pushed up from the counter.

"Oh?" Cadence challenged. "And just who are the right men then?"

Hayden came in close. "I think you know the answer to that."

"How can I know for sure, Hayden?" She searched his eyes. "I've known Ryan since childhood. I thought I knew him well, but I was still blindsided. And now you're here and you're so similar to each other. How can I know you won't treat me the same way?" Her heart was racing so hard she thought it would pound right out of her chest as she waited for his answer. She desperately wanted to give into the pull she felt towards him, but she didn't want to be hurt again.

"Ah, Cadi." He slipped one hand onto her cheek; stroking his thumb over her cheekbone. "I could deny that I'm a womanizer until I'm blue in the face, but it wouldn't convince you. You're going to have to decide that for yourself. Can you trust me? Have I ever given you reason to doubt me?"

Cadence gulped. "I looked you up, Hayden."

He stiffened. "What do you mean?"

"The more I got to know you, the more I felt confused. In the kitchen you were hard as nails, but outside, I was seeing a much different man. So I looked up your backstory. I know about New York."

Hayden's hand dropped, and he took a step back. "You do, huh? That remains to be seen. There are two stories about what happened in New York."

Cadence nodded. "I figured. The article I found wasn't very complimentary, but I also noticed it never gained much traction. If it's alright with you, I'd like to hear your side."

Hayden's eyes narrowed. "Why do you care? It seems to me that you're just looking for evidence that I'm just like that Ryan guy."

Cadence took a deep breath and gathered her courage. Resting her palm against his stubbled cheek, she whispered, "Or maybe I'm looking for reasons that you're not."

Several breaths went by before Hayden nodded. "Come on, I'll talk while we cook." Hayden turned back around to the supplies he had on the counter.

Walking to the sink, Cadence washed her hands then joined Hayden. "What first?"

"Put two cups of water in this." Hayden handed her a pot.

"Right. Two cups." She glanced around for the measuring cups then grabbed what she needed.

"Nope! That one is for dry ingredients. Use this one." Hayden shoved a glass with a handle into her hands.

"Really?" Cadence raised an eyebrow. "You use different measuring cups for the same measurement in different ingredients? Doesn't that seem inefficient?"

Hayden gave her a push toward the sink. "I can tell you the science behind it later, right now, get to it. I'm starved."

"Aye, aye, Captain," she grumbled.

"Works for me," Hayden said with a grin.

"It would. I thought you were going to tell me what really happened in New York."

After putting the pot on the stove and turning on the burner, Hayden showed her a cutting board. "You're gonna chop these veggies, then we'll sauté them." He sighed. "Truthfully, there's not much to tell. My boss was a woman who enjoyed all the perks that went along with being a prominent businesswoman in New York. She owned one of the best restaurants in the city and I was on top of the world when she hired me straight out of culinary school." He grinned at her. "I know I've said it before but I was one of the youngest head chefs in the city and considering it was New York, well, that's saying something."

Cadence hummed her agreement, waiting for him to continue.

"In my exultation, what I didn't pay attention to was how often she switched out her head chefs. I was too excited to finally be out doing what I loved." He eyed her still hands. "Come on, you gotta work while I'm talking."

Cadence eyed the massive knife she had been provided. *I'll be lucky if I get out of here with all my fingers intact.*

Awkwardly, she began to slice the produce she had been given.

"Stop! You're going to lose a finger."

Cadence huffed. "I told you I don't know any of these things, perhaps you need to actually teach me." She stuck out her bottom lip.

"What are you, like two?" Hayden came up behind her and reached his arms around. He put his hands over both of hers and demonstrated how to chop without hurting herself.

Cadence couldn't breathe. His warm chest was at her back and his deep voice too close to her ear. She could feel his breath against the side of her face and knew it would take very little effort to turn and taste those incredible lips once again. *Focuuuus, Fooocus. Cadence! You have a knife in your hands! FOCUS!*

"Cadi," he whispered against her ear. "It's your turn to try."

"Kill me now," she said under her breath.

Hayden chuckled behind her and she nearly dropped the knife. *Oh my word, I really am going to take off a finger.* Her hands were shaking ever so slightly as she gripped the sharp utensil and did her best to replicate the actions he had shown her.

"Better, keep practicing," he said right before kissing her on the cheek and stepping away.

Cadence's mouth dropped into an 'O' shape and she froze. Her cheeks were warm, but the spot he kissed was tingling. *Oh. My. Goodness. I'm as bad a teenager with her first crush.*

"Are you done, yet?" Hayden barked from across the kitchen.

"Sorry, almost." Cadence finished as quickly and safely as she could. "Here." She carried the board over to him.

Hayden glanced at her work and frowned. "You'll learn, I suppose."

Cadence rolled her eyes. "Charmer."

"Yeah, I get that a lot." He walked over to the stove. "Water's boiling. Come on."

"You haven't finished the story."

"Yeah, we'll get there. Just a second. One cup." He handed her a dry measuring cup and the bag of couscous.

Cadence slowly took them from him. "Okay, and what? Put it in the water?"

"Good one, Einstein."

Cadence scoffed. "Careful, I'll end up with a head as big as yours." She scooped out the small, hard granules and poured them into the bubbling water.

"Admit it, you like my head." He smirked. "Now quick, turn off the stove, stir, then cover with a lid."

Cadence sped through his directions then jumped back with her hands in the air. "Done!"

"Nice. We should time you for the cooking rodeo."

"They time things at a rodeo?"

"Are you kidding me? You haven't been to a rodeo, either?" He put his hands on his hips. "Just what kind of childhood did you have?"

One where I was raised by nannies and private schools and never learned to do anything for myself. "I grew up in California, Hayden. I lived in the city. Why in the world would I have gone to a rodeo?"

"I'm sure they have rodeos in California."

"Maybe so, but not in L.A."

"Fine, I'll give you that. Now come on, we have work to do."

They spent the next fifteen minutes cooking down the vegetables and chicken. After everything was cooked, Hayden helped her mix them together.

"This isn't nearly as hard as I thought," Cadence said as they put all the dishes on the table.

"Hey, hey, hey! Don't downplay what I do!" Hayden exclaimed as he set their dishes on the table. "Cooking is an art form, so it's definitely hard. It requires skill and artistic ability, but that doesn't mean there aren't things you can cook that aren't chef level." He pulled out her chair for her. "You might not be Picasso, but you can still finger paint," he whispered in her ear after pushing her in.

She worked to hold in the shiver that ran down her spine, but after glancing up to see a grin on Hayden's face, Cadence knew he had noticed. "Your confidence in my abilities is astounding."

Hayden shrugged then began dishing them both up. "Eh, you crunch the numbers, I crunch the produce. It works."

Cadence leaned in and took a bite. "Ooh, nice! I've never had couscous quite like this before."

Hayden paused with his fork in the air. "You've eaten couscous?"

"Of course," Cadence said nonchalantly.

"Huh. I'm surprised."

She frowned and put down her fork. "Why?"

"Because you didn't grow up in a cooking household. It's not usually the type of food you find unless you have someone who knows what they're doing in the kitchen."

"Oh." Cadence didn't know how to respond. She didn't want to tell him of her background but the fact that she was lacking so many life skills was catching up to her.

"Look, it's no biggie. Forget I said anything." He put a large bite in his mouth.

"Besides, we aren't talking about me. We're talking about your boss who has a penchant for hiring chefs."

Hayden swallowed and cleared his throat. "Right. Well, it became very clear after working for her for a few weeks that she was after more than my talents in the kitchen."

Cadence's hand holding her fork dropped to the table with a clang. "Oh."

"Yeah." Hayden pursed his lips and nodded. "Oh." He let out a harsh breath. "I didn't take it too seriously. I tried to avoid being alone with her and just did my job. Between her business skills and my cooking, that restaurant was one of the 'must see' places in New York. We were thriving."

"So what happened, then?"

"I kept turning her down." He shrugged and picked at his food. "I assumed that eventually she'd get the message and move on to someone more willing. Instead, she got angry. One night, she gave me two options. I could hold on to my morals or my job."

Cadence gasped. "That snake! That's completely illegal. How could you let her get away with that?"

"Whoa there, Tiger." Hayden grinned. "It all turned out alright."

Cadence gave a small laugh. "I suppose you're right."

"So, just to finish it off. When I still said no, she used her connections to cut me off from the entire food community in the city. The only places I could have been hired would have been a fast-food joints. And no offense to those who work there, but that's not what I had in mind when I went to culinary school."

"Well, I'll admit I've never had something this good at a fast-food restaurant."

"Can't take all the credit, you helped," he said in between bites.

"What?" Cadence put her hand on her chest and gave her best southern belle expression. "Why, Sir, are you finally giving glory to someone else? I do declare, I never thought I'd see the day."

"Ha! Keep it up, Cadi. I tried out a new dessert recipe last night and if you're nice, I'll let you try some."

She narrowed her eyes. "Does it involve chocolate?"

He leaned over the table. "And peanut butter."

Cadence snapped upright. "Yes, Chef. Thank you, Chef. Very good, Chef."

Hayden laughed and shook his head. "Glad we got that cleared up."

Cadence grinned while she ate. *This is turning out far better than I thought.*

HAYDEN KEPT HIS HEAD down, but watched Cadence through his peripheral vision. She was stunning in her relaxed state. *Almost as beautiful as when she's angry.* He thought back on what she had told him when she first arrived and his anger flared just as before. *What kind of idiot treats a woman that way? Especially Cadi? Unbelievable. No wonder she was so prickly when she arrived.*

Cadence sat back with a satisfied sigh. "I don't think I can eat another bite," she groaned. "I'm going to gain twenty pounds if I keep eating your food."

Hayden stood, taking his plate to the sink. "I guess that's just more chocolate for me, then."

"Don't make threats you can't keep, Hayden," Cadence said as she followed him. "Have you ever witnessed what happens to a woman when you deny her chocolate?"

"Can't say that I have," he said over his shoulder.

"It's not pretty. Think of a hangry man, but with sharper claws."

"I'm shaking in my boots."

"You're not wearing boots."

He glanced down. "Huh. I could have sworn I felt some kind of tremor."

Cadence frowned and shook her head. "I can see I'm going to have to let you experience it first hand."

Hayden couldn't resist the opening. Now that she was finally opening up to him, he intended to take full advantage. Stepping into her personal space he leaned down close. Close enough to smell the citrusy perfume that she wore. He was tempted to just close his eyes and savor the scent, but there were other things to take care of first. "Probably for the best. Some people learn best through hands on experimentation."

Her chest rose and fell rapidly and her eyes dropped to his lips before popping back up. "That's true. What type of person are you?" Her voice was lower than usual.

Slowly his hand rose until it slid along her neck. Her hair was heavy and soft. Cupping the back of her head, he pulled her forward until their lips were only millimeters apart. "I'll let you guess," he said huskily before closing the gap.

Unlike their first kiss, this one was slow and calculated. Hayden reached his other hand up until he framed her face with his hands. He slid his lips along hers, tasting and pecking, until she reached out and wrapped her arms around his waist, pulling herself in closer. Taking that as a sign of acceptance, Hayden tilted her head and deepened the kiss. He slid one arm down her back and pulled her in close.

Time became lost as they explored each other and the chemistry that was unfolding between them. She felt right, perfect even, in his arms. *This is exactly where she belongs.* The permanent status that thought represented shocked Hayden and broke his concentration.

Haltingly, reluctantly, he pulled back. "Cadi," he said in reverence. He peppered kisses across her face as he ended their exchange.

"Hmm?" She kept her eyes closed and her head tilted back as he continued to caress her soft skin.

"We need to stop."

"I know," she murmured in her low, alto voice.

Letting go of her, he stepped back and stuffed his hands in his pockets to keep from reaching for her again. It took a few heartbeats for her eyes to flutter open and the sight caused Hayden to duck his chin and grin up at her from under his lashes.

Cadence's eyes widened and her trembling fingers rose to her lips. "I-I can't believe we- it was-" She blinked rapidly and her sentences were fragmented and halting.

"I know," he stated. "Me too."

Cadence stopped stammering and looked straight at him. Her blue eyes warmed and a small smile crept onto her face.

Tension and attraction hung thick in the air, nearly igniting in its intensity and Hayden knew he had to break it up or he'd go after her again. He cleared his throat and took a step toward the kitchen. *When in doubt, offer food.* "I believe I promised you chocolate."

Cadence's shoulders relaxed. "You did and I aim to see you keep it. I'll bet doing the dishes will help us work up an appetite."

Hayden stopped his progress and blatantly looked her up and down. "I don't think having an appetite is a problem."

Cadence's cheeks flared up again, and she delicately cleared her throat. "Guess I walked into that one," she said with a rueful grin.

"True enough," Hayden laughed. "Come on, let's clean up."

Twenty minutes later, they settled on the couch with bowls of peanut butter mousse pie. "You know," Cadence said around a mouthful, "you're not nearly as scary as you want everyone to believe."

Hayden raised an eyebrow, and he pulled the fork out of his mouth, not speaking until after he swallowed. "Maybe you just haven't spent enough time around me yet."

"Are you now trying to convince me that I should stay away?"

Hayden leaned over and gave her a quick peck. "Never." He could see her fighting a grin and he found himself smiling in return. "I have to work tomorrow night, but if you'll come eat at the restaurant, I'll come say 'hi' and deliver your food personally."

"Hmm..." Cadence playfully narrowed her eyes at him. "Would kisses be included with my meal?"

"Only if you order the daily special."

Cadence giggled then sobered. "Oh. I forgot." She scrunched her face.

Hayden's heart dropped. *Uh oh.* "What?"

"I have..." Her eyes darted away from him and his nerves ratcheted up even higher, "Well, there's no way to really get around saying this. I have a date."

Hayden's hands settled in his lap. "You have a date?"

"Yes," she said softly. "It was planned a week ago."

"So cancel it."

She tilted her head. "Hayden, I can't just cancel it. That would be rude."

His eyebrows shot down. "So is going out with someone other than the person you're dating." *Does she not feel the same way I do? Did that kiss not mean anything to her?*

Her eyes shot to his. "Is that what we're doing? Dating?"

"What did you think we were doing?"

Cadence rolled her eyes. "Well, it's been a little hard to tell. Mostly we fight and then you ply me with food and amazing kisses. Not exactly what a woman thinks of when she imagines dating someone."

Hayden shrugged nonchalantly. "So our methods are unique. Our relationship is ours and no one else's. Who cares if we're a bit unconventional?"

"Still," Cadence set down her bowl on the coffee table, "when I agreed to the date, you and I were still at odds. The best thing to do would be to go and tell Oliver in person that I'm involved with someone else."

Hayden choked. Setting down his bowl, he fought to catch his breath.

"Hayden! Oh my word, stay calm and breathe." Cadence whacked him on the back a couple of times, then started rubbing in a soothing manner. "Are you okay?"

He nodded as he wheezed. When he could finally swallow and take a full breath, he sat upright and looked at her. "Oliver? Are you seriously telling me that you are going out with OLIVER?"

Cadence frowned. "Don't shout at me. I told you I agreed to this before you made your feelings clear."

Hayden fell back against the couch cushions. "That guy was a complete loser! He used a handkerchief for heaven's sake!"

Cadence stiffened. "Maybe he's into being green. You know, less trash and all that."

Hayden turned and looked at her. "Cadi, did you or did you not see him wipe his forehead with the same piece of cloth he blew his nose on? Multiple times! I almost had him kicked out as a health hazard! And have you forgotten that he was just using you to get to Eli?"

Cadence laughed and pushed his shoulder. "You did not. And stop being mean. He apologized about that and promised not to do it again. Now ease up. He was the first guy to show any interest in me this last year."

Hayden growled and pulled her close. "That's not true."

She grinned. "Okay. Let's put it this way. He was the first guy to ask me out in a way that actually appeared genuine. Fighting with me all the time did not in any way shape, or form make me think you liked me."

"Not sure why," he kissed her jawline. "Little boys do that all the time. Didn't anyone ever pull your pigtails at school?"

"Are you telling me you have the wooing technique of a five-year-old?" Cadence ran her fingers through his hair and Hayden closed his eyes to enjoy the sensation.

"I'm just saying it's a tactic as old as time. Not to mention how attractive you are when you're all worked up and the fact that you're so easy to rile."

She laughed and shook her head while continuing to play with his hair. "Only with you. No one else has the ability to drive me crazy like you do."

"Let's keep it that way," he said as he leaned in for a sweet kiss. "So, you'll cancel with Oliver?"

"No," she whispered against his lips. "But I will tell him I'm unavailable."

Hayden pulled back. "So you'll come to the restaurant?"

She kissed him on the nose. "No. I need to tell him in person."

Hayden frowned. "Why can't you just be like everyone else and give me what I want? My staff is much better at obeying than you are."

Cadence laughed. "If you had wanted that, you should have dated one of your workers. Besides, someone has to keep you grounded. Your ego is entirely too big all on its own. You need someone who can pop it once in a while."

"Yeah. His name is Nelson," Hayden grumbled good naturedly.

Cadence laughed again, then shifted and snuggled into his chest. Hayden automatically wrapped his arms around her and pulled her closer.

"I'm not ready to go home yet. Can we watch something?"

Hayden did a mental fist pump. "Sure." He pushed her upright, so he could grab the remote, then settled back down with her tucked up against him. "Anything in particular?"

"How about the Food Network? I've always had a thing for Mario Batali."

"So now the truth comes out. You just want me for my cooking skills."

She nodded her head. "Absolutely. Especially the chocolate desserts."

Hayden laughed and kissed the top of her head. "Wanna scroll through my Netflix account?" He offered her the remote.

"Perfect," she murmured.

CHAPTER 13

Cadence tapped the table in a nervous pattern as she waited for Oliver to arrive. *It's not like there was really anything between us. We didn't even really have a first date, so this shouldn't be a big deal at all.*

"Sorry, I'm late," Oliver said as he slid into the other side of the booth. "Ended up on a phone call I couldn't get off of." He smiled.

"Not a big deal," Cadence reassured him.

"Have you already ordered?" He picked up the menu in front of him.

"Um, no. I wanted to say something first." Cadence felt her heart rate pick up and her back felt damp. They might not have been dating, but telling someone you wouldn't be seeing them again was hard no matter what.

"Oh?" Oliver set down the menu and gave her his undivided attention.

"I uh, well see I'm-"

"Is this about last week, again? I said I was sorry. I shouldn't have tried to use you to speak to Mr. Truman." He frowned. "I thought we cleared this up already."

"No, no, no. This isn't about that at all."

"Then what is it?" He pulled out his hanky and wiped his brow.

Cadence nearly laughed as she thought of Hayden's description of Oliver being a health hazard. "You see, some things have changed in my life this week and I'm... well, I'm seeing someone."

Oliver just stared at her.

"Oliver." Cadence tilted her head down to make sure he understood her. "I've started dating someone else. We had planned this date before my relationship became official, so I thought it would be best to let you know in person."

"You're dating someone?"

"Yes."

"Is it that chef guy? The rude Truman brother?"

"Oliver! That wasn't very nice." Cadence frowned at his anger.

"Yeah, well neither was his breaking up our date last week."

Ooh. He wants to point fingers does he? "A date which you had already broken up because you admitted to using me."

Oliver threw his hands in the air. "I said I was sorry."

"And so did he."

"I never heard him," Oliver sneered.

"Maybe not, but he apologized to me and that's good enough."

"Until he figures out you're only after him for his money."

Cadence gasped. *Where is this coming from? And they say a woman scorned is bad.* "I am *not* just after him for his money. In fact, his money is one of the main reasons I have been holding off on dating him." She forced her voice into a whisper even though she wanted to shout.

Oliver folded his arms. "Guess you changed your mind. Flashing a little bling will do that to people. What did he do? Buy you a new pair of shoes?"

"Hello, folks! Have you decided what you would like to eat this evening?" A young man held a pad and pen at the ready.

"No, thank you." Cadence said as she gathered her purse and slid out of the booth. "I've lost my appetite." *Good riddance.* Cadence thought as she stormed out of the restaurant.

Once in the car, she turned the vehicle toward the resort. "Maybe I'll take Hayden up on that offer for dinner after all."

Once she arrived, she parked in the back where employees left their vehicles. "No point in taking up a spot for a regular customer," she murmured as she got out and headed toward the building.

Just as she was walking past the back corner of the kitchen, on her way to the front, movement caught her eye. Glancing over, she froze. Hayden's white chef's coat stood in stark contrast to the dark building. In front of him was the same waitress Cadence had seen running out of his office the other day.

What's going on here? Images of Ryan and his secretary flooded her mind, but Cadence forced herself to remain calm. *He isn't doing anything... yet.*

Stepping into the shadows, Cadence watched as Hayden handed a bag to the young woman. The waitress beamed and spoke excitedly for a moment before Hayden nodded. Then she reached out and touched his forearm.

No. It can't be. Please say this isn't what it looks like.

Moments later, the woman had left and Hayden headed inside. Cadence leaned her back against the building and put her hand to her heart. "They didn't do anything. They didn't do anything." She chanted the words over and over again. "If he were cheating, wouldn't he have hugged or kissed her or something?" She slid down until she was crouching on the balls of her feet. "Come on, Cadence." She squeezed her eyes shut. "You know better than anyone that things are not always what they seem. Ryan is a prime example." An ache formed in her heart and she rubbed at it.

"No." She stood and threw back her shoulders, blinking back the tears before they could fall. "Hayden has given you no reason to doubt him. He didn't touch her, he didn't do anything but give her a sack. Just ask him. You're an adult. That's how adults handle things in the real world. They stay calm and ask questions when necessary."

Forcing her breath to stay even and her walk to stay casual, she finished walking toward the front of the building.

"Hello, Ms. Everwood!" Bethany greeted her. "All alone tonight?"

"For now," Cadence said with a forced smile. "Is it busy inside?"

"About normal, but the main dinner rush is starting to wane, so this is perfect timing." The young blonde grinned. "Let's go grab you a seat."

"Thank you," Cadence said as she followed the hostess, then again as she tucked herself into a booth.

"Anytime!" Bethany bounced back to the front, leaving Cadence by herself. Her thoughts swirled, and she had to repeatedly keep herself from getting up and leaving.

"Hello, Ms. Everwood. How are you this evening?" Evan, one of the regular waiters, stood at the end of her table.

"I'm fine. Thanks." Cadence gave a small smile. "How are you?"

"Doing all right, thank you. The rush has slowed down so that makes my evening a lot easier."

"I'll bet."

"What can I get you tonight?" He grasped his hands behind his back as he waited for her answer.

"Water with lemon, please. And then if you'll just tell Chef Truman that Cadence would like the special, please."

Evan gave her a quizzical look. "Sure thing. I'll be right out with that water."

Cadence nodded her thanks and settled in to wait. *Should I have said that? What if there's more to what I saw? What if-*

"Hey, Beautiful!" Hayden slid into her booth and gave her a lingering kiss.

"Hayden!" Cadence pulled back and looked around. "We're in public."

"So? That's what a booth is for." He grinned and leaned in again.

Cadence gave a small laugh as he kissed her again. For a moment she forgot all about what she had seen.

"What happened to Oliver?" Hayden smirked. "Decide he wasn't worth the time?"

Cadence's happiness came to a screeching halt. "No." She looked down at the table. "I uh, decided it was best to explain and just leave."

"Hey," Hayden tilted up her chin. "Don't feel bad. You got the better end of the deal."

Did I? "Hayden, I wanted to-" She stopped. *How will it sound if I accuse him of something? He didn't actually do anything. It was probably, hopefully, completely innocent.*

"What's wrong?" Hayden frowned. "Did Oliver give you a hard time?" Hayden pushed a hand through his hair. "I knew that guy was bad news. After what he pulled last week-"

"Hayden!" Cadence put her fingers over his mouth then sighed when Hayden kissed them. "It doesn't matter now. Now, you promised me a good dinner if I came. You better get back in the kitchen and get it done, Mister. Chop, chop."

Hayden laughed and kissed her cheek. "Yes, Chef. Of course, Chef," he teased as he scooted out of the booth. "Right away, Chef..."

Cadence smiled and shooed him away.

Only moments after he was gone, Evan arrived with her water. "Thank you, Evan," she murmured.

"You're welcome." He paused before leaving. "So, uh, you and Chef, huh?"

Cadence froze for a split second. "Yes." She said finally. "Me and Chef."

Evan smiled and nodded. "Cool. I'll be out with your dinner soon."

Cadence thanked him as he left. *See? No one else sees any red flags. If he was having a relationship, Evan would have said something. Right? It's nothing, I'm sure.*

Pulling out her phone, Cadence scrolled through her social media feed as she waited for her food.

HAYDEN FLEW THROUGH making Cadence's dinner. He had been completely caught off guard when Evan had informed him she was here. *Good thing, though. I was ready to march over to where she was eating and take Oliver's head off.*

He'd been distracted all evening, thinking about her sitting down with that guy. *What if he had tried to kiss her or something?* He growled. "I'd have knocked his block off."

He flipped the sautéing vegetables. "She's mine." The words were out of his mouth before he thought better of it and the strength of them brought him to a halt. *Whoa. Time out there, Romeo, you've barely started dating.*

With a grunt, he went back to preparing her dinner. His mind wandered as he worked the familiar motions and he thought about Rebecca. She had shown up a little early, but he had still filled a couple of styrofoam containers full of food and brought them out to her. She had been so thankful and Hayden had been tempted to offer her information on other resources she could use, but he was afraid of offending her.

He huffed. *Since when have I ever been afraid of offending someone?* He grinned. *Since Cadence came around. I better be careful or I'll get too soft.*

He finished her dish and glanced around the kitchen. His workers were like busy little bees, everyone absorbed in their own worlds.

"James!"

"Yes, Chef?"

"I'm taking a break in the dining room. Take over."

"Yes, Chef. Thank you, Chef."

Hayden held onto the hot plate and walked over to Cadence's table. He nodded at patrons he was familiar with along the way, but never stopped as he made his way to his destination. Knowing that Cadence had come and was waiting for him was like a drug and he wanted more.

He'd been angry a lot as a kid, many bullied kids were. But then he'd learned to channel that anger. And when football was over, he'd channeled it into his cooking and now his kitchen. So, the light and airy emotions traveling through him were completely foreign. *And I don't even care.*

"Cedar plank salmon for my lady," Hayden said with a flourish as he placed the plate in front of Cadence.

"Mmm... oh my word, that smells delicious." Cadence closed her eyes and took in a long sniff.

Hayden settled in beside her. "It's always best to eat something while it's hot. Never tastes as good when it's cold."

Cadence shoulder bumped him. "Maybe so, but a few moments of reverence never go amiss."

"True enough." He fought the temptation to puff out his chest when she finally took a bite and moaned.

"Soooo good." She glanced at him while she cut another bite. "I think I might keep you around."

Hayden cocked the side of his mouth up in a crooked grin. "I don't know. Maybe I should find someone who wants me for more than my cooking." He frowned when he noticed her stiffen. "Hey, I was just joking. We already established it was the desserts that drew you in, right?"

She laughed, but it sounded forced. "Right."

What was that all about? He waited to see if she would say anything more, but she went back to eating and didn't speak.

"I hate to say it," he slapped his hands on the table, "but I've got to get back to the kitchen."

Cadence gave a commiserating smile as she chewed.

"What are you doing later? I can be out of here in about an hour and a half."

She swallowed. "Nothing, I guess. Tomorrow's the weekend, so I can stay up a bit."

"I'll make it worth your while," he leaned in and whispered against her cheek before kissing it.

"Oh yeah? How are you going to do that?" Her eyes twinkled in the candlelight and Hayden found himself completely mesmerized by her.

"I was thinking we could have another lesson tonight-"

He grinned when she started to groan and he gave her a peck to stop the complaining. "And make something sweet."

Cadence perked up. "Can there be chocolate involved?"

Hayden rolled his eyes. "You do realize there are lots of desserts that don't have chocolate in them, right?"

Cadence shrugged. "There might be, but that doesn't mean they're worth eating."

Hayden snorted a laugh. "I guess I'm just going to have to change your mind on that."

"I look forward to it," she whispered.

"I'll text you when I'm on my way home." With one more kiss, he slid out of the booth and headed back toward his kitchen. He fought hard to put his usual scowl on his face rather than the smile that wanted to stay plastered there. *Still got a kitchen to run, Idiot. Get it together. Even if you will be counting down the moments until you see her again.*

CHAPTER 14

"No! Wait!" Hayden started coughing as Cadence dumped the flour into the moving mixer.

"What the heck was that?" Cadence fanned the air around her and coughed. "Does that always happen?"

"If you dump a bunch at once, yes," Hayden growled. "You've got to shake it in a little at a time. Like this." He stepped up behind her, took a hold of her hand and showed her how to tap the measuring cup on the edge of the mixer, shaking the flour in slowly. "Much better," he murmured in her ear.

Cadence's internal temperature skyrocketed, and a shiver ran through her. "Would have been nice if you'd told me that to begin with," she snapped back.

Hayden chuckled against her back. "And miss seeing you all covered in flour? Not a chance." He kissed her cheek, then let go and stepped away. She immediately missed his touch.

"So, I take it you didn't ever help your mom make cookies when you were a kid either? Did you just eat store bought ones?"

Cadence bit her lips. "So, what's next?" She asked, keeping her eyes on the mixer.

Hayden leaned his hip against the counter next to her and folded his arms. "Why do you always clam up when I ask your childhood? Was it really that bad?"

Cadence felt her cheeks heat and knew they were turning a dark pink, but she still didn't answer.

He reached out and ran a knuckle against her warm skin. "Come on, Cadi. You can tell me."

Cadence batted her eyelashes. "Tell you what? There's nothing to tell."

Hayden sighed. "Fine. Keep lying to yourself that's fine."

Cadence closed her eyes and pinched the bridge of her nose. "Look, Hayden, I'm not ready to go there yet. I've already told you more than I've told anyone else, but we're just barely beginning this relationship... thing. Am I really expected to just pour out all my deepest, darkest secrets?" *Especially when you're keeping some yourself? Cadence!* she scolded herself immediately. *You didn't see anything happen, so let it go.*

Hayden grinned and stepped forward. "So you admit we're in some kind of relationship?"

"Seriously? That's what you got out of that?" She put her hand on her hip. "You know, for a guy who has such a large ego, you sure need a lot of reassurance. And I thought we established the other night that we were dating."

He shrugged nonchalantly. "We did. It's just nice to hear you admit it." He leaned into her cheek. "Warms this cold heart to hear the words from your lips."

She could feel him grin before kissing the edge of her mouth. "You keep teasing me and you might regret it, Mister."

"Sounds like we need to get a little sugar in your system. It works wonders to tame the beast within." He winked.

Cadence fought the smile tugging at her lips, but she lost miserably. "You are so naughty, Hayden Truman."

"Eh, it's part of my charm." He stepped away from her. "Now, come on. Let's get these cookies in the oven."

"Cookies. Right." Cadence bustled around following Hayden's instructions.

After the cookies were in the oven, they settled on the couch with a movie, curling into each other.

"That timer sure seems to be taking forever," Hayden frowned and looked at his phone. "How long did you put it on for?"

"Ten minutes, like you said." Cadence mumbled as her eyes stayed riveted to the screen.

"Give me a sec." Hayden stood, displacing Cadence, and turned to walk into the kitchen. "Ah, crap! Open the windows! Quick before the alarm goes off!" Hayden rushed around waving a kitchen towel through the air, trying desperately to break up the cloud of black smoke billowing out of his oven. A burnt smell began to permeate the house.

"Oh my goodness! What did I do?" She ran over and started tugging on the nearest window. "Dang, your windows are heavy," she grunted.

"Here," Hayden shoved the towel in her hands and pushed the largest window up himself.

Cadence took up the task of waving away the smoke while Hayden grabbed a hot pad and took the ash cookies out of the oven. Marching to the front door, he walked outside and dumped them in the woods.

Cadence was coughing when he came back in. "Well, on the plus side, I think it's starting to dissipate."

"Way to look for the silver lining, Sunshine."

Cadence folded her arms and stared him down. "Well, excuse me, Mr. Grouchy Pants! Maybe if you had explained the timer a little better on your crazy, complicated oven, we wouldn't have this problem in the first place!"

Hayden shot his eyes toward the ceiling. "Heaven save us from nutty, pyrotechnic women."

The embarrassment surging through Cadence was overwhelming. She didn't know whether to cry or scream or both. Instead, she chose the 'get the heck out of here' route. Ducking her head, she headed towards the door.

"Whoa, whoa, whoa! Where do you think you're going?" Hayden grabbed her around the waist as she tried to walk past him.

"Home!" she mumbled. "Back where no one makes fun of me or mocks my attempts at cooking. Back where I'm the only one who sees when I botch something up."

"How boring is that?" Hayden lifted one side of his mouth in a grin."Aww, come on, Cadi. It'll be alright. I shouldn't have teased you so much. I'm sorry. Usually you love it when I tease."

"No, I don't," she mumbled into his shoulder. Despite being upset, his touch was comforting, and she wrapped her arms around him and pulled him close.

"No one likes to fail, Sweetheart. But it's not the end of the world."

Cadence leaned back and blinked a couple of times. "This coming from the man who demands perfection in his kitchen?"

He shrugged and tucked her under his chin. "We're not in my kitchen, or at least not my professional kitchen. I mean, come on. So, you botched the cookies. Do you know how many cookies and cakes I burned before I got through culinary school?"

Cadence huffed. "What? You didn't just demand they obey and cook perfectly?"

"Believe it or not, desserts don't have good listening skills."

In spite of herself, Cadence found a giggle bubbling through her lips. "Okay, how many?" She tilted her head so she could look at him.

Hayden's eyebrows rose. "What?"

"You wanted me to guess how many cakes and cookies you burnt. I'm asking for the answer."

Hayden scrunched up his face and stared into space for a moment. "Let's see, there was that time in second grade-"

"What? You were cooking in second grade?" She dropped her head back on his shoulder. "You're not making me feel better."

"Oh, I'm sorry. Was that what I was supposed to be doing?"

Cadence rolled her eyes and when she stepped back, he let her. "Come on, it's getting late and you promised me sugar."

"That's right, I did." Grabbing her hand, he tugged her in and gave her a lingering kiss.

"Mmm…" Cadence hummed as he pulled back. "That might actually be better than chocolate."

"Careful. You'll inflate my already oversized ego." Hayden started walking toward the kitchen. "Why don't you grab a pen and paper so you can write down the instructions on how to work the timer."

Cadence stopped and looked at him wide-eyed. "Is it really that complicated?"

Hayden burst out laughing. "Not for most of us, but you've proved you don't fall in that category."

That smile tugged on her lips again. "Jerk," she muttered, punching him in the arm.

"Yep. Now, come on, I'm hungry."

TWENTY MINUTES LATER, they both sat down on the couch again and restarted the movie. A contentment Hayden wasn't used to rushed through him. *Now I understand why Eli was such a mess when he and Ivy were getting to know each other. How the heck am I supposed to handle all these feelings? How do women do it?*

"Oh, my gosh," Cadence leaned down and took a long sniff of the plate sitting on her lap. "These smell sooo good."

Hayden smirked. "You can admit it's me you're smelling. I won't tell anyone."

Cadence snorted. "Not hardly." She took a bite and groaned. "Good grief, I have finally lived."

Hayden shook his head. "I can't believe you've never had a peanut butter chocolate chip cookie before."

Cadence put her hand over her mouth. "And I can't believe you cook things like cookies."

Hayden frowned before taking a bite. "Why?"

Cadence shrugged, and she polished off the treat in her hand. "I dunno. It just seems so below your pay grade or something."

Hayden pointed his half eaten morsel at her. "According to my mother, cookies are a way of life and anyone who tells you differently is selling something."

Cadence raised her eyebrows. "I think you're the one trying to sell me something."

Hayden grunted, but didn't argue. "Next time, we'll have to try not burning the first batch."

Cadence huffed. "I'm never going to live that down, am I?"

Hayden pursed his lips and shook his head. "Nope. It's too much fun to tease you and see your cheeks turn all pink."

"Whatever," Cadence grumbled. She finished off another couple of cookies before turning on her phone. "Ah, shoot. It's late. I gotta get home or I'll be a walking zombie in the morning."

"Tomorrow's Saturday. I'm pretty sure you can handle anything in front of you with your eyes closed."

Cadence shot him a look. "Well, I suppose you can rest assured that I wouldn't bother coming after you if I was hungry then."

Hayden barked out a laugh. "Cadi, you say the best things. I never know what I'm going to get with you."

Cadence grinned and picked up another cookie. "I really shouldn't, but I really want to." She looked at it.

Hayden took the plate from her lap and set it on the coffee table, then reached over and grabbed Cadence around the waist. Pulling her in, he tucked her back up against his side and wrapped his arms tightly. "Go ahead, just live a little," he whispered in her ear before giving it a light kiss.

"As long as you know what you're getting into when I roll out of here ten pounds heavier." Cadence wiggled a little to snuggle in deeper and let out a contented sigh.

"Cadence Everwood. You are the most beautiful woman I have ever met, so quit trying to convince me otherwise."

She stiffened and slowly pulled forward so she could turn and look at him.

Hayden was shocked to see her eyes were glistening. *Crud. What did I do?*

"Do you really mean that?" she whispered.

"Of course." He scrunched his face and shook his head. "Don't you know me enough by now to know that I don't say things just to be nice?"

Cadence audibly swallowed. "Yes. I guess so. It's just. No one has ever said it to me that way before."

Hayden's eyebrows furrowed. "What do you mean 'that way'?"

"Well, I've been told I'm beautiful before. But usually it comes with something else, like, that dress makes you look beautiful. Or that new haircut really brings out your eyes. Or, wow, losing those five pounds really made a difference."

"Unbelievable," Hayden growled. "Are your parents still living? Because, seriously, I'd like to give them a piece of my mind." *What kind of house was she raised in?*

Cadence faced forward and snuggled back into his arms. "Yes, they are, but your words wouldn't matter. They're pretty stuck in their ways."

"Why won't you talk about them?" Hayden asked softly as he ran his fingers through her hair.

There was several moments of quiet before Cadence spoke. "I'm worried you'll want nothing to do with me if you knew about what things were like before I got here."

Hayden frowned and thought about that for a minute. "I think there are very few things you could have done that would drive a wedge between us, Cadi. Are you hiding a husband back home?"

"No," she stated emphatically.

"A criminal record?"

"Of course, not!"

"Are you just after me for my money?"

"NO!" Cadence shot upright and turned to look at him. "I absolutely am not after your money. Please believe me."

"Okay, calm down. I was just throwing out scenarios." Hayden turned her and brought her back into his arms. "Since you've answered everything in the negative, I don't really see what could be so bad."

She sighed. "It's not really me that was the problem. Or, not directly anyway. Let's just say that I had an experience that opened my eyes to parts of my parents' lives I wasn't privy to before. I decided I couldn't live that way, so I took my stuff and left."

"Huh. Are you still in touch with them?"

"Sort of. Mostly we argue over the phone about when I'm coming back."

Hayden gave her a little squeeze. "Did you tell them you found the most amazing man ever, and that's why you're staying here?" He nuzzled the top of her head.

Cadence laughed. "Truth be told, I don't think that would convince them. But nice try."

"You never know. I know how to schmooze if necessary."

"Thanks, but I'm not ready to cross that line yet." She sighed. "Let's just watch the movie, huh? Then I need to get home and get some sleep."

Hayden let the subject drop, but he couldn't help wondering what had happened. *Maybe it's time I did a little research on her the same way she did with me. I'm falling harder and harder for this woman and there's something she's not telling me. I need to know.*

CHAPTER 15

Hayden woke up to a pounding on his door. "What now?" he grumbled, rolling out of bed. He held onto the door frame for a moment to catch his bearings before stumbling down the stairs. "I'm coming, I'm coming. This had better be good."

"Hayden!" Nelson's voice called. "Open up, Man! I forgot my key!"

Hayden swung the large, wooden door open. "What in the world are you doing banging my door down at..." he glanced at the wall clock, "six in the morning? Some of us don't rise with the sun, you nincompoop."

Nelson burst out laughing while he shouldered his way inside. "Nincompoop? Is that the best you could come up with? Obviously your brain doesn't rise with the sun either."

"Whatever," Hayden growled as he padded into the kitchen to start the coffee maker. "You better have a good reason for being here. I stayed up late last night."

"Yeah, I noticed."

Hayden frowned and turned around to look at his brother. "What is that supposed to mean?"

Nelson pushed something on his phone, then set it on the counter.

Not again. Hayden walked over and glanced at the screen, then did a double take and picked up the device. There, clear as day, was him sitting with Cadence in the booth at his restaurant, kissing her. Hayden was used to the public limelight. Even before he and his brothers found the treasure, he had had a certain level of status as a chef. But now that Cadence was involved, for the first time he felt violated and dirty. *Why do people think that someone's private moment is fodder for their social media feed? Is nothing sacred any more?*

"Someone posted a video, and it's gone viral," Nelson said softly. His hands were tucked in his pockets and he rocked back and forth on his heels.

Hayden growled and put the phone on the counter. "This is none of their business. Why can't people just leave us alone?"

Nelson shrugged. "Really, you kissing a woman isn't that big of a deal. Celebrities are caught doing that kind of thing all the time. It's what people are saying about Cadence that is the problem."

Hayden rounded on Nelson. "What do you mean? What are people saying about her?"

Nelson rubbed the back of his neck. "I'm kinda afraid to tell you. Most of it isn't complimentary." He narrowed his eyes at Hayden. "And it brings some questions up about who she is."

Hayden felt like he'd been socked in the gut. "What do you mean?" When Nelson didn't answer right away, Hayden's temper blew. "Just say it! What's going on?"

Nelson sighed. "People are calling her a two-timing cheat. They claim she's engaged to some big-wig lawyer down in California. The Everwood family is apparently heavily involved in politics and she's basically California royalty."

All the blood drained from Hayden's head and his vision swirled. He stumbled forward and held onto the counter's edge. *I should have looked her up. I should have followed my instincts and looked her up.*

"Dude, you all right?" Nelson grabbed him by the shoulders and gave him a little shake.

"Did you say she's engaged to some guy down in California?" Hayden asked hoarsely.

"Well, that's what people are claiming, but we know better than anyone that what they say online isn't always right."

"Right." *Keep it together. Nelson's right. You need to find out from Cadi what's going on.* Hayden took a long breath in through his nose and pushed it out his mouth. The only sound for the next few moments was his forced breathing. The breathing wasn't calming his anger the way he hoped it would. Grabbing the phone, he began to read through the comments. It didn't take long to catch the gist of the story. The simmering inside of him turn into a full boil. "I need to speak to her."

"You sure you're up to that? I'm not sure ripping her head off is the way to go here. Especially the woman you're in love with. You mess this up and you won't get her back."

"Who says I'm in love with her?" Hayden growled. "We've only been together a few days, technically."

"Dude, you two were destined from the first moment you shouted at each other."

"Whatever." Hayden shoved away from the counter and headed toward the garage.

"Where are you going?" Nelson scurried after him.

"Cadi's."

"Okay, Man. Be careful though, huh?"

Hayden nodded and grabbed his keys on the way out. Jumping into his sports car, he tore down the winding gravel road all the way to Cadence's little cabin. He stormed up to the front door and pounded so hard it made his knuckles sting.

The door swung open "Hayden! What in the world?" She looked over his shoulder and glanced around. "Is something wrong?"

"You might say that." He tapped his fingers on his thigh. "Can I come in?" he asked when she didn't say anything.

"Yeah. Sure. Sorry." She stepped back and opened the door wider.

Hayden stepped in just far enough for her to close the door. She kept her back to him for a few moments before turning to look at him. "Would you like to sit down?" she asked quietly.

"No, thanks. I'd rather stand."

She pursed her lips and nodded. "'Kay. I think I'll grab my coffee if that's all right?"

Hayden nodded.

Cadence patted the large bun on top of her head. "I wasn't expecting visitors. You caught me before I really had a chance to dress or anything."

For the first time, Hayden noticed that she was in pajama shorts and a t-shirt, her hair wadded up and no makeup on her face. *And she's still gorgeous.* His stomach fell. *Please say the news isn't right. Nelson's right. I love her. I don't want to lose her.* "This won't take long," he grumbled.

"Oh. Okay. What can I do for you?"

"I just have one question. Are you engaged?"

Cadence choked on the coffee she was sipping. Turning to the sink, she spit the rest into the drain and caught her breath. "What did you just say?"

Hayden's handed clenched and unclenched. *Her reaction says it all.* "I think you know," he said in a low voice.

The fire that Hayden loved shot through her blue eyes and turned them to ice. "No. I don't think I know. I just want to be very sure that I heard the man I'm dating or the man I *was* dating, accuse me of leading him on while I was engaged to someone else."

"A video of us kissing in the restaurant last night went viral."

Cadence's eyes widened.

"Apparently, the Princess of California is stepping out on her fiancé."

"What did you call me?" Her face paled.

"Once again, you heard me. What I want to know is why you didn't tell me? How many times have I asked about your family and past and you just pushed it away?" He shoved his hands into his hair. "All this time I've been falling in love with you and you had a fiancé at home!"

"I DO NOT HAVE A FIANCÉ!" Cadence shouted over his angry mutterings.

Hayden closed his mouth and stared at her.

"You want to know everything? Fine. I'll tell you everything. I was raised with a silver spoon in my mouth. My life was cushy and easy, a total bubble. I lived in a grand mansion and my mother never set foot in the kitchen unless it was to give orders to the cook."

"Well, that explains why you don't know your way around a kitchen."

Cadence's lips pinched into a thin white line. "My father is a lawyer who eventually made his way into the political arena. We were the perfect family. Or so I thought. My mother was beautiful and elegant and always looked perfect in the spotlight. She and Dad smiled at all the right times and drew attention wherever they went. I was the obedient, dutiful daughter who always followed two steps behind. People starting calling us the royalty of California." She snorted and plopped into a chair. "You know what the worst part was? I was content. I was happy. I thought we really were the perfect family." She lay her head back with a sigh. "Anyway, once their perfect, little princess was of age, I became engaged to a man I had known my whole life. Ryan Woodward."

Hayden growled and shook his head. Turning, he went to grab the doorknob.

"Oh, don't leave now, Hayden. The story isn't done yet." Cadence's sarcasm was so thick it could be cut with a knife. "The best is yet to come, as they say."

Hayden turned around and folded his arms over his chest. "By all means..."

"Thank you, Chef." Cadence gave a sarcastic grin, which fell only moments later. "Ryan was everything my father wanted. A lawyer with an interest in politics. Handsome, wealthy and charismatic. Everything dear, old Dad could groom into the perfect son-in-law and reach even further in the political game. And naïve, little me agreed to the plan." Her voice got quieter. "I didn't love Ryan, but we were friends and I assumed that with time, we would reach the same type of marriage my parents had. Perfect." She paused, her gaze turning to her hands, which were clasped tightly in her lap. "Only it wasn't perfect. Once day, I went to surprise Ryan and take him out to lunch and found him with his secretary. They were occupied in… non-business-related activities."

Hayden's jaw nearly hit the floor. "What?"

"After confronting him and returning the ring, I marched home, sure in my righteous anger that my decision would be backed by my parents." Her eyes traveled to the window and a lone tear made its way down her cheek.

Hayden's anger had started to wither, and he desperately wanted to know what had happened. "Please keep going," he said softly.

Cadence nodded and brought her eyes back to him. "My father tried to convince me it was no big deal. That Ryan had some wild oats to sow and when age and time caught up to him, he would eventually be faithful."

"You've got to be kidding me."

"Nope. And best of all, he then admitted that he had had multiple affairs and proceeded to let me know that my mother knew about them. When I confronted her, she told me they didn't matter, because she had the lifestyle she wanted."

"No wonder you were so aloof when you got here." He shook his head. "What kind of parents would put their child in that position?"

"Ones who care more about their image and power than their child's happiness," she murmured. "Really, I should have seen it coming. I mean, I was totally being groomed for it, but I just thought that all the clothes and hair and shopping were my mom's way of showing she loved me. They paid for my education, but then never allowed me to use it." She massaged her forehead with her fingers. "I let myself believe they thought I would be happier staying at home like my mom. And I wanted to be. I wanted to be just like her."

Hayden huffed. "Be thankful you aren't."

Cadence jumped out of her seat. "How would you know? You obviously don't know me at all. Bursting in here accusing me of using you to cheat on someone else."

Crud. How do I fix this? He put his hands out to the side. "Look, Cadi-"

"Especially when you keep your own secrets." She threw up her arms. "Once again, I should have known better. But nope! I believed it was all okay. And instead, I traded one cheater for another. Once again, I'm not good enough to be first in someone's life."

HAYDEN JERKED BACK as if she had slapped him. "What are you talking about? I haven't cheated on you. You're the only woman I've had an interest in in years!"

As soon as she had said the words, Cadence knew they were wrong, but she was so angry that she had been unable to hold them in. *In for a penny, in for a pound.* Her eyes narrowed, and she stalked toward him, poking him in the chest. "I'm not so sure about that. I saw you behind the kitchen the other night. You were with that waitress. The same one who was coming out of your office crying."

Hayden cocked his head. "Oh yeah? And just what did you see? Was I involved in 'non-business like' behavior?"

Cadence's voice softened, and she swallowed. "No. Which is why I haven't brought it up. I was trying to give you the benefit of the doubt, but now that you're accusing me without proof, it's hard not to do the same."

Hayden's whole body seemed to deflate. "You're right. I haven't been completely honest in regards to the waitress."

Cadence's heart fell. *Unbelievable. I really did do it again. I fell for a man who doesn't feel the same. How could I have been so stupid?* Tears pricked her eyes, and she backed up. "I get it. No need to explain." She started to turn, but Hayden grabbed her arm.

"No. There's every need to explain. I can't tell you everything, because her information isn't mine to tell, but I will tell you that what you saw was completely innocent. I was giving her a couple packages of food. That's it."

Cadence's eyebrows furrowed. "You were giving her food?"

He nodded. "Yes."

"Why does she-"

Hayden held up a hand to stop her. "I told you I can't tell you her story. That wouldn't be fair. But I can promise that's all it is."

Cadence studied him. Her heart wanted to believe, but everything was so messed up right now. She wasn't even sure what she was feeling. Hurt that Hayden had accused her of cheating. Relieved that everything was out in the open. Embarrassed and angry at having to relive the story of her family. And hope that Hayden wasn't actually involved with anyone else behind her back.

"What are you thinking?" he asked, staring intently at her.

"That I'm not sure what to think or feel right now."

Hayden nodded and looked down. "Yeah. I didn't really start us off on the right foot here, did I?"

"Truthfully, it's a relief to have it out." Cadence wandered back to the kitchen and grabbed her now cold coffee. She poured it out and started a new pot, then turned and crossed her arms. "Of course, your storming in here like a man ready to kill someone wasn't how I envisioned it going, but still."

"Yeah, well, you thinking I had cheated isn't any less painful."

Cadence sighed and stared at him sadly. "So where do we go from here?"

Hayden started towards her. "I'm thinking we kiss and make up. Isn't that what most couples do when they have their first fight?"

Cadence dropped her chin and glared at him. "First of all, that was absolutely not our first fight. We have bickered since we first met."

"Only because you won't just admit I'm right all the time."

She rolled her eyes. "And I never will, so maybe we need to just cut our losses now." Pain pinched her heart at the words, but after such horrible accusations, how could they possibly keep going forward?

Hayden paused only a foot from her. "You don't mean that."

Cadence threw up her arms. "I don't know what I mean. We can't just go back to the way we were. Both of us have said nasty things to the other, and you just found out I come from a Stepford-type family. Doesn't that negate what you said earlier?"

He took another step closer but didn't touch her. "What did I say earlier?"

"That you were falling in love with me." Cadence's voice had dropped to a quiet, vulnerable sound. *Isn't there supposed to be roses and chocolate when a guy confesses to loving a woman? Why is my fairytale so horrible?*

"I don't think that's what I said," he hedged.

Her eyes widened and heat shot straight up her neck. "You're going to deny-"

Hayden pressed his fingers to her lips. "I believe what I said was, I *am* in love with you."

Cadence felt her lip tremble as tears filled her eyes once more, only this time for a different reason. "Do you really mean it?"

He ran a finger down her cheek. "Did you mean it when you said you were falling for me?"

She bit her shaking lip and nodded her head.

"Then what do you say we let go of what happened today and move forward, huh? We both made a mistake. It happens. Let's learn from it and move on."

"Are you sure? My family is still pressuring me to come home and marry Ryan. Leaving home hasn't taken that away."

He froze. "Do you want to marry him?"

"No," she choked out and gave a light laugh. "Absolutely not."

Hayden cupped her face. "Then I don't see what the problem is. You're an adult and just because your parents want something doesn't mean they get it. They can't force you to marry him. Right?"

"Right." She smiled. They stood smiling at each other in a rare moment of peace. The tension in the room began to thicken and pop and finally, Cadence could stand it no longer. "I think this is the point where you're supposed to kiss me."

"Thank heavens," Hayden mumbled as he bent down and took her mouth.

Cadence sighed into the kiss and leaned into him. Just as she was wrapping her arms around his neck another banging came from the door.

They jerked apart. "Who in the world could that be?" Cadence wondered as she walked over to let them in. "Nelson! What are you doing here?"

"Is Hayden still here? Or did he tick you off and get sent packing?"

Cadence laughed. "He's here. Come on in."

"Hey, Bro! Glad to see you're still alive." Nelson grinned as he waltzed in.

Hayden folded his arms and glared. "What do you want now?"

Nelson put his hand on his chest. "I'm thinking you should be thanking me. Looks like you and the lady have worked things out, so you should be grateful I brought all this junk to your attention."

Cadence walked past Nelson and stepped in next to Hayden, putting her arm around his back. Hayden copied her action and tucked her in close. "I can't say I loved having him think I was two-timing him, but it is good to have it all out in the open."

Nelson shined his nails on his shirt. "Yeah, well. If you're happy about that, then you should be really happy with me for finding this next bit."

"Just spit it out, Nelson," Hayden growled.

Nelson's face fell. "Actually, to be honest, this part isn't so good." His eyes went to Cadence's and her stomach dropped. "Your family has put out a statement in response to the video."

She felt her knees go weak and Hayden tightened his hold. "What did they say?" she whispered.

"They're saying that it's all a big misunderstanding. That you and Ryan had a tiff, and you were getting back at him, but that you are working everything out and the wedding will proceed as planned."

"What?" Cadence screeched. Her eyes shot up to Hayden's angry face. "There is no wedding! I broke up with Ryan a year ago. They're completely delusional. I haven't even spoken to Ryan since I got here, no matter how many times he's called."

"He's been calling you?" Hayden asked incredulously.

"Well, yeah. I mean, it would be weird if he hadn't called at all, right?" Cadence frowned.

"But he's still calling, even this much later?"

Cadence rubbed her throbbing forehead. "Yeah. I've never actually answered his calls, so he just keeps calling."

"Have you spoken to anyone from home?"

"I told you I've spoken to my parents. They keep trying to get me to come home and proceed with the wedding, but I keep telling them no."

"Is it possible that they've told Ryan that you're still going to marry him?" Nelson jumped in.

"I suppose, but Ryan is smart. He has to know what's going on. He's probably only calling so he can say he has. He doesn't love me. He's just looking forward to the prestige of marrying into my family." Cadence closed her eyes for a minute. "Nelson, can you show me what you saw? I need to see exactly what they're saying and how."

"Yep." He glanced around. "Don't you have a remote here?"

"Yeah, just a sec." She pulled it out from a basket, but Hayden pulled it out of her hands and set it back.

"Let's go to my house. I've got a better system than you and we can check all the news stations."

"'Kay."

It only took moments for them to load into their cars and drive through the woods to Hayden's home. Once inside, Hayden turned on one of the twenty-four-hour news stations. It only took a minute or two for the story to be aired again.

"In other news, Cadence Everwood, dubbed the Princess of California, has been caught sneaking a kiss with someone other than her fiancé. In fact, it proved to be none other than one of the 'Overnight Billionaire Bachelors', Chef Hayden Truman.

"Now, Ms. Everwood's family has made a statement declaring that all is well. They claim that Ms. Everwood was simply getting revenge after a fight with her intended, Ryan Woodward, but from the looks of that video, I'm not sure people believe it. Meanwhile, no one has been able to get ahold of Ms. Everwood for her own statement."

Hayden muted the television.

Cadence sat on the couch in stunned silence. "This is so ridiculous. I've kept quiet because talking to the media would prove my parents to be liars and it would absolutely ruin my dad's career. I might be mad at them, but I'm not trying to run him into the ground." She gave a loud huff as she fell into the back of the cushions. "Why can't people just mind their own business? I'd still really like to see a clip of my family's statement."

"Give it time. They're cycling the story everywhere and eventually the video will pop up again." Nelson said from the kitchen where he was raiding the fridge.

"It's funny that they said people have been trying to get a hold of me." She glanced at her phone. "I haven't heard from anybody, not even my family."

Nelson's phone rang, grabbing everyone's attention. "Uh, oh," he murmured before answering it. "What's up, Big Bro?" Even from the couch, Cadence could hear whoever was on the other side of the line shouting, but she couldn't make up the words. "Chill! We'll take care of this! ... Yeah. I know. ... Yeah, she's actually here with us... No, we're at Hayden's house... Got it. Yep... Yep... 'Kay. Bye." He hung up and put his head back in the fridge.

"Nelson," Cadence said with forced calmness. "I think you'd better tell us what's going on." Hayden had sat down beside her and she could feel the tension radiating off of him. *He's gonna lose it if Nelson doesn't speak up.* She rolled her eyes. *Although, I think Nelson does this on purpose.*

"Yeah, hang on." He grabbed the container he wanted and shut the fridge door. After he had also supplied himself with a fork, he sauntered over to the conversation area and plopped down in a recliner.

"Nelson, I swear I'm going to-" Hayden started.

"Yeah, yeah." Nelson waved his fork through the air. "Well, Cadence, either no one knows your phone number, or they thought it would be better to simply talk to you in person, because the castle is completely surrounded by paparazzi. In fact, Eli is calling the police as we speak."

Cadence gasped.

"People can't get in or out and the restaurant is being hounded as well." Nelson took a large bite. Once he had swallowed, he continued. "So, we decided it would be better if you stayed here for a while."

"What have I done?" she murmured. The weight of everything that had happened and was still happening, suddenly became too much. Tears trickled down Cadence's cheek and a sharp ache radiated from her sternum. She felt as if the despair would swallow her whole. *If I had just stayed home and followed through with what my parents wanted, nobody would be in this mess.*

"Don't do it, Cadi," Hayden growled. He reached over and took her shoulders, forcing her to look at him. "This isn't your fault. I don't care who your parents are, they have no right to demand you marry anybody. Especially not some jerk who will cheat on you and take you for granted. You are way more than just a trophy wife."

"But your resort and your customers." Cadence sniffed and blinked to stop the tears. "It's my fault everything is a mess right now. Those reporters are here because of me. Eli said everything is blocked. They're going to drive your patrons away and then people will start leaving nasty things online about the situation." She put her face in her hands. "I should have just married Ryan."

"Hey, Nelson," Hayden said in a deep, angry voice.

"Game room is mine!" Nelson jumped up and hightailed it out of the great room, disappearing down the hall.

Cadence wiped her tears as she watched him go. "What was that all about?"

"He knew I needed a few moments with you," Hayden stated. He put his hands on either side of her face. "Cadi. I want you to hear me loud and clear. I've never been good with sentimental junk and I'm probably not going to start now, which is why I don't want to have to repeat this again. Got it?"

Cadence nodded.

"I love you. You caught me completely off guard when you showed up in Eli's office and I haven't been the same since. I think I've been falling in love with you from that first moment we snapped at each other, even if I did spend the first year just trying to make you angry." He put his forehead to hers and chuckled. "I couldn't help it. You are magnificently gorgeous when you get upset and I've always had a thing for a woman with fire."

Cadence gave a watery laugh. "Yeah well, all that did is make me think you were an arrogant jerk. Even if I was attracted to you, it made me so angry that I couldn't get rid of that."

He kissed her forehead. "I have never backed down from a challenge. And I always-"

"Get what you want. Yeah, yeah. I've heard that before." Cadence rolled her eyes playfully.

"Good. Lesson learned. Now." He pulled back so he could look into her eyes again. "You are worth the fight, Cadi. I don't care who we have to go up against or what kind of lies your parents are spewing. I'm not giving you up. I love you. You're the missing piece of me and I refuse to let you go."

Her face scrunched as she went into 'ugly cry' mode, but for once, Cadence didn't care. "I love you too," she whispered through her tears. "And I don't want to go back. I want to stay here with you."

"Sounds perfect." Hayden leaned in gave Cadence an achingly sweet kiss.

Oh... my... goodness... how did I ever get a man like this?

When he pulled back, Cadence almost followed him, not ready to give up his touch. But she knew now was not the time to get carried away.

"Come on, Sweetheart. Let me feed you." Hayden stood and held out his hand.

She wiped her tears with one hand while taking his with the other. "Will there be chocolate?"

"For you? Always." Hayden kissed her fingers then led her into the kitchen where he proceeded to make the most perfect chocolate chip pancakes ever.

CHAPTER 16

Hayden was starting to feel like a caged tiger. All day he had stayed at home with Cadence, which was wonderful, but he hated leaving his restaurant for so long. The thought that he wasn't there to oversee things was driving him crazy, but according to Eli and Ivy, the reporters were still too thick to handle.

The police had broken up the outside mobs, but they couldn't stop people from coming into the restaurant, if they were willing to act as a customer.

"At least we're getting money out of them," he muttered as he worked on dinner.

"What was that?" Cadence was on the other side of the kitchen chopping lettuce and she glanced over her shoulder. "Am I doing it wrong again?" She looked at the leafy vegetable and frowned. "I'm probably the only person in the world who can't even chop lettuce correctly."

Hayden barked out a laugh, some of his tension easing with her pouting. Walking over, he pecked her on the cheek. "You're doing fine. I mean, it doesn't matter if the lettuce is actually chopped or, you know, massacred, we'll still eat it."

"Jerk," she muttered with a grin, before throwing a piece at him.

Hayden reached out and caught it, then stuffed it in his mouth. "See? I didn't die."

Cadence rolled her eyes and went back to working on the salad.

Picking up his wooden spoon, Hayden stirred the pasta. Eli, Ivy and Nelson were all coming over so they could brainstorm how to handle the situation and he was going to feed everyone dinner. Spaghetti and meatballs was not only simple, but comforting as well, just what the group needed tonight.

"Mmm." Cadence put her nose in the air and took a big sniff. "That bread smells soooo good." She looked at him with a smile. "Do you think you could teach me how to make bread some day?"

"I'll teach you anything you want," Hayden said with a smile. "But not until you stop killing my greens." His shoulders shook with silent laughter as he heard her muttering something under her breath. *I probably don't want to know what she said.*

A knock sounded at the door before it opened. "Hello!" Eli's voice rang through the great room.

"In the kitchen," Hayden answered. Grabbing the pot in front of him, he took it to the sink and dumped it in a colander to drain the water from the pasta. After putting the pasta back in the pot, he went to the stove and started mixing in the sauce.

"Smells good in here," Ivy's sweet voice said as she, Eli and Nelson all made their way into the house. Ivy went straight to Cadence and grabbed her in a hug. "How are you holding up?"

Cadence was several inches taller than Ivy and she had to bend down in order to hug the petite woman back. "I'm all right. Hayden talked me off the ledge earlier. Right now I'm mostly frustrated and sad."

"That totally makes sense," Ivy responded as she let go and stepped back. "I'd be the same way. I think it'd be hard for anyone to have their family using the media against them."

Cadence nodded but didn't speak. Hayden kept an eye on her out of his peripheral vision. She'd gone from one extreme to the other all day long and he wanted to help her when he could. *And if holding her and letting her cry into my shoulder helps her feel better, then I can't say I object to such an action.*

"Oh, how the mighty have fallen," Eli laughed as he slapped Hayden on the back.

Hayden raised an eyebrow. "What exactly does that mean?"

"You're growing soft, Old Man," Eli whispered in his ear with a chuckle.

Hayden shoved him with his shoulder. "You're one to talk. You've been whipped for months."

"Yep! And proud of it." Eli's smile was wide as he pumped his eyebrows a couple of times before walking back to where the women were chatting.

"Let's get everything on the table," Hayden announced as he pulled the bread out of the oven.

Everyone grabbed something, and they all headed to Hayden's extra long dining table. Once settled, they said grace and started filling their plates.

"So," Hayden swallowed the bite in his mouth, "what's the latest at the castle?"

Eli and Ivy looked at each other before Eli answered. "The police are keeping the crowds off the property. Things are running smoothly for the most part. However, individuals are still sneaking in. The restaurant has had an hour wait all day. The phone lines haven't stopped ringing. And we've had an unusual amount of people asking to speak to management."

Cadence hung her head. "I'm so sorry, everyone." She sniffed. "I had no idea that this would happen."

Hayden grabbed her hand and gave it a squeeze, which brought her head up. She gave him a grateful, but watery smile.

"I thought when I left home, I was leaving those problems behind. I mean, my parents still pestered me on the phone but I continued to turn them down. Ryan even called several times, but I never picked up. I just kept thinking eventually they would get the message." She let out a long breath.

Ivy leaned forward over her plate. "I don't mean to seem rude, but I'm afraid I only know bits and pieces. Would you mind filling us all in?"

Eli and Nelson nodded their agreement with the request.

"Sure, if you really want to hear it. I just hope you all don't hate me after you know."

Hayden wrapped an arm around her shoulders and pulled her in close so he could kiss the side of her head. "Nobody is going to think any less of you, Cadi. The bad guys here are your parents and Ryan, not you."

"All right." With a deep breath, she filled the rest of the group in on her back story. Ivy gasped and scowled at all the appropriate times, but Eli and Nelson simply listened and absorbed.

"So," Cadence put her hands out to either side, "there you have it. All the nitty, gritty details."

"Why do you think they're working so hard to get you back? I mean, why do they really care if you marry Ryan or not?" Eli asked as he took another bite of bread.

Cadence sighed. "I think it all comes back to the politics of it. Our family has quite a bit of power already, but Ryan is younger than my dad, and he's a rising star. I think by pulling Ryan in as a son-in-law, my dad thinks it will give him more power. He can use his own experience to push Ryan farther than he managed himself. And then my dad would get the benefits of that, being related and all." She squished her mouth to the side. "And honestly, I think my mom is behind a lot of it. She came from a poor background and has made it clear she will never go back to that kind of lifestyle again. She wants the power and prestige this marriage would bring probably as much or more than my dad does."

Everyone nodded.

"Have you spoken to your parents since this all went down?" Ivy asked quietly.

Cadence shook her head. "No. I figured if they wanted to say something, they would have called."

Ivy chewed her lip for a moment. "Would you be willing to call them?"

"Fairy girl, you got something up your sleeve?" Nelson grinned and wiped his mouth.

"Maybe." Her eyes trailed back to Cadence. "But I think first, we should try talking to them and see what they say. It might even be best to talk to Ryan. Maybe he doesn't really want all this drama and would help you end it."

"I hadn't thought of that," Cadence murmured. "I've been too upset about everything to think rationally, I guess."

"Why don't we finish eating and then we can grab your phone, hmm?" Hayden said.

"Is that your solution to every problem? Throw food at it?" Cadence smiled fondly at him.

"Hey, if it works, it works. Never knock the power of calories." *Or men who are fighting for their woman.*

CADENCE HELD HER PHONE with trembling hands. Everyone had gathered into the seating area and were watching her.

"Hey." Hayden leaned over and spoke into her ear. "We're all here to help, so we absolutely don't want to make this worse for you. Do you want to make the call in private?"

Cadence shook her head. "No. I think I need you here."

"Okay, then I'm here." He took her closest hand. "Put the call on speaker and that way we can all try to figure this out, alright?"

She took a steadying breath. "Alright." Turning on her phone, she tapped a couple of buttons and pushed send. The phone only rang twice, but it felt like an eternity before someone picked up.

"I figured you would come to your senses," her mother's low voice carried out of the speaker. "You have embarrassed this family long enough. When can we expect you?"

Hayden squeezed her hand and Cadence was so grateful for the support. "I'm not coming home, Mom. I called so we could try to end this once and for all."

"I don't understand how you can be so ungrateful! We have given you everything! Everything! And now we're handing you a handsome, wealthy husband who, if we're lucky, might even make it into the White House, and you're throwing it all away."

"Mom, I-"

"Do you realize how much work we have gone through to put all this together? And how difficult it has been to keep the media from realizing the truth? For a year now we've let you test your wings. I thought it might help you realize how good you had it here, but your stubbornness knows no bounds, apparently."

"Mom, if you would just-" Cadence tried again.

"I don't know where we went wrong. You never lacked for anything and all we've asked is that you marry Ryan. One little thing. You've been destined for that very purpose since you were a young girl and now you're throwing it all away. All for some, some restaurant worker! Unbelievable. If you wanted to have someone on the side, you can certainly do that after you and Ryan are married, but not before. If people suspect-"

"MOM!" Cadence's temper got the best of her. She had been holding it together until Arianna had started in on Hayden. Attacking the man Cadence loved was not going to be tolerated, mother or not. "I will not listen to you insult Hayden that way. He's done nothing wrong. I think what you're forgetting here is that I'm a grown woman and I have my own opinions on how my life should go. I don't love Ryan and I don't want the kind of life you and dad have set up for me. I want to do things on my own. I like working and I enjoy living on my own."

Her mother huffed. "Maybe your father can talk some sense into you." The phone made a shuffling sound before her father's voice came online.

"Hey, Cadi-Bear."

"Cadi-Bear?" Hayden mouthed while scrunching up his nose.

"Knock it off," Cadence hissed back, pushing him with her shoulder. As frustrated as she was, his light laughter helped break up the tension in the room. Cadence glanced at everyone's faces and was surprised to see sympathy pouring from every individual. *How come these guys are so sweet, but my family is a pain in the tush?*

"Hey, Dad," she answered.

"I understand you're still being difficult."

Cadence closed her eyes and sighed. "I'm not being difficult, Dad. I have told you from the very beginning that I'm not coming back to marry Ryan. There has never been any other answer. It's you three who are holding onto this pipe dream."

"Now, sweetheart, we've been planning this for most of your life. Just think of the things we can do once you and Ryan are married. His name is already plastered all over the state and when you combine it with ours, he'll be a shoo-in for the first election."

"Dad," Cadence groaned. "Once again, you're not listening to me. I'm not going to marry him. You need to just tell the news the truth. We broke up ages ago and I'm happy with that. Don't you want me to be happy? I don't love Ryan!"

"Nobody said you have to love him. You just need to appear in public like you do. It's not that hard. He's handsome and charismatic. I hear women enjoy men like that," he chuckled. "Love is overrated anyway. It comes and goes. Ryan can keep you in the same lifestyle you've grown up in and you can have everything your little heart desires."

"You're not listening to me!" Cadence's voice rose, but she pulled it back down when Hayden squeezed her hand again. "I'm happy where I'm at. I have no desire to move back to California."

"Surely you're growing tired of that tiny little cabin you're living in. Why, the thing looks like it would fit in your bedroom back home."

Cadence froze. "How do you know what I'm living in?" Even though she had spoken over the phone with her parents, she had never told them exactly where she was living or working. She was afraid they would show up and ruin things for her.

Her father chuckled. "Sweetheart, do you really think I wouldn't keep tabs on where you were and what you were doing? I've had a man following you since you first jumped into your little sports car."

Cadence felt the blood drain from her head.

"Cadi," Hayden grabbed her shoulders and turned her toward him. "Cadi, breathe, Sweetie. It's going to be okay."

"That the guy you've been hanging around? I understand he's some kind of billionaire." Her father whistled. "I must say, you do know how to pick them. If we hadn't already gotten Ryan all set up in his career, here, I don't think I'd mind adding those kinds of funds to the family."

Hayden's face turned red, and he snatched the phone from Cadence, ending the call. "Come here," he said to Cadence, pulling her shaking form into his embrace.

"I didn't even know. I've been followed this whole time, and I didn't know." She buried her face in his chest. "How could I not see this? How was I fooled for so long?"

"They're your family, Cadi. Who expects their family to be a bunch of social climbing jerks?"

"That's one way to put it," Nelson grumbled. "What?" He asked when Eli slapped the back of his head.

Cadence huffed a laugh. "No, he's right. That was definitely a nice way to describe them."

"Cadence, sweetie, I'm sorry to ask this of you, but I think you should try Ryan," Ivy said softly.

"I'm pretty sure we know all we need to know," Hayden growled as he tightened his hold on Cadence.

Ivy shook her head. "I know it's hard, Hay, but maybe Ryan isn't a willing participant either. If she can get his help, we might be able to put a stop to her parents' machinations."

"Well, that's a ten-dollar word," Nelson quipped from his recliner.

"Dude. Are you ever serious?" Hayden asked incredulously.

"Not if I don't have to be. Someone has to keep the stress from strangling us all to death," Nelson said with a cocky grin.

Hayden opened his mouth to speak but Cadence spoke up. "No, it's all right, Hayden. Nelson is trying to help and Ivy has a point. Maybe Ryan can see reason here."

"I don't like it," he whispered, putting her forehead to his.

"I don't either," she whispered back. "My emotions feel like they've been through the garbage disposal, but we've got to end this. We can't keep hiding. You have a restaurant to run and the people at the resort shouldn't have to deal with all these reporters swarming the area."

He sighed and his shoulders fell. "You're right, but I don't like seeing you hurt."

Cadence grinned and leaned in for a small peck. "I guess you'll just have to kiss it better, then."

Hayden raised a brow and moved to close the gap again, but Cadence leaned back. "Later," she mouthed with a wink.

Hayden turned to glare at Nelson who was snickering behind his fist while Cadence picked her phone back up.

"Here we go," she said firmly.

"Cadence! Is that you?" Ryan's normally suave voice sounded frantic and Cadence felt a small pang of remorse at her treatment of him.

"Yeah, Ryan. It's me."

"Are you okay? Are you ready for me to come get you?"

Her eyebrows furrowed and Hayden's body stiffened next to her. "Um, I'm fine. I don't need you to come get me. Why would I want you to do that?"

Ryan blew out a long breath. "I've just been worried, I guess. Your parents kept telling me that you just needed time but you never answered my calls. When that video surfaced, I wasn't sure what to think. Your mom is insistent that the wedding is still going to happen. She and my mother are almost done with all the planning, in fact. Don't you want to come help out with the details?"

Cadence crinkled her nose. "Ryan, I left because I wanted out of everything back home. And I've stayed gone because I like it here."

"But what about the wedding?"

"Ryan. I gave the ring back. There is absolutely no wedding. I called that off when I left."

"I know but... your mom says you didn't mean it. I mean, I get that it wasn't great you caught me with my secretary, but it was just a little kissing. Aren't you over that by now? It's been a year. That kind of stuff is no big deal. We have a plan. We've always had a plan. We can't change it now."

Cadence put her hand on Hayden's chest as he lunged for the phone, a fierce anger on his face. "It was a big deal, Ryan. That's not the kind of marriage I want. Look," she closed her eyes and pinched the bridge of her nose, "I have no intention of coming home and marrying you. My mother and father don't seem to want to hear those words, but there they are. I don't love you, I never loved you as more than a friend and I don't think you felt any differently about me. Correct?"

"Well, no, but we-"

"No, Ryan. Let's just say it like it is. Truth is, I *am* in love now. The guy in the video is the right guy for me and I want this media storm to go away. Are you willing to help me do that or not?"

A long pause occurred, and the room seemed to collectively hold their breaths.

"I don't know, Cadence. Your family name is a huge boost to my career. Our marriage will put me way ahead of the competition. I don't really want to let that go. Not to mention I'm not sure we can stop our mothers at this point. I think they've got the venue booked for next month."

Cadence sucked in a breath. *Unbelievable.* "Listen carefully, Ryan. I'm in love with someone else. Do you really want a wife who you have to force to marry you? One who wants to be with someone else? I mean, seriously. What kind of life is that? We both deserve better."

"Ryan, if I may?" Ivy piped up.

"Who's that?" Ryan asked.

"Ivy is a friend of mine from my job," Cadence said, then nodded to Ivy.

"Ryan, I think if you worked it right, you could use this whole thing as a boost, anyway."

"What do you mean?" Ryan's voice was clearly skeptical.

"Well, think about it. A man who has just been deeply wounded by his fiancée, but finds the power to continue pursuing his career because he believes so strongly in what he is doing. The news will be all over that. Not to mention all the extra talk about who they think you might marry. You'll be in the media for weeks. And you know what they say, any publicity is good publicity." Ivy grinned and winked at Cadence.

Holy cow, I think Ivy missed her real calling in life.

Cadence wasn't the only one who thought so as Eli was looking at his wife like she had grown a second head. Ivy shrugged coyly at him and leaned back in her seat.

"Duuude, you're messing up my claim as the most devious mind here, Tiny One," Nelson fake whispered.

Ivy rolled her eyes and shook her head.

"I actually think that might work," Ryan said. "But you're going to have to do something big, Cadence. The kissing video has people up in arms, but with your parents still claiming we're getting married, people will simply mark it off as a drunken night on the town."

"Oh, don't worry," Ivy called out. Her arms were folded over her chest and a smug smile played on her lips. "I've got just the thing."

CHAPTER 17

"You can't be serious!" Hayden yelled after Ivy had told the whole family her plan. Jumping up from the couch, he began to pace. Not two minutes ago, they had ended their phone call with Ryan and now Ivy was throwing this bomb at them.

"I'm dead serious," she said stubbornly. "It's the only way. If Cadence is married to you, then her parents can't get to her. It cuts them off once and for all, plus it lets Ryan have his jilted story, which will allow him to make his way without Cadence's influence."

Hayden pushed his hands through his hair. "You've lost your mind, Ivy."

"Watch it," Eli said in a dark voice. "That's my wife you're talking to."

"Well, then you keep her crazy ideas in check!" Hayden waved an arm at them.

Eli jumped up, his fists tight and his face red. "She's trying to help, Hay. Now, either calm down or go take a hike. You're not helping things right now."

"Neither is she!" Hayden got in Eli's face. His frustration was roaring, and he had the insane urge to punch something. Or bake. Either way. *When Cadence and I get married, it won't be because we were forced to.* "Cadence's parents have already been trying to force her to get married and now you're asking me to do the same. I won't do it."

"Hey, Hayden," Nelson tapped Hayden's shoulder, but Hayden brushed him off.

"Not now, Squirt."

Eli put his hands up in a placating gesture. "I get it, but this time, we're only pushing things forward that were bound to happen, anyway. You love each other, right?"

"Hayden," Nelson tried again.

"Seriously, Man, not now!" Hayden shrugged him off again. "Yes, we love each other, but it's too soon. We haven't actually been a couple that long."

"No, but you've been dancing around each other for months." Eli laughed. "It's longer than Ivy and I were together."

"Well, who's fault was that?" Hayden rolled his eyes.

"Hayden, you really need to listen," Nelson said harshly.

"What?" Hayden turned toward his younger brother and threw up his hands. "What can't wait for just a few minutes while I pound some sense into Eli?"

"Go ahead and try, Idiot," Eli muttered.

Hayden shot him a dark look before putting his attention back on Nelson.

"I think you should take that walk Eli mentioned."

"What?" Hayden shook his head. "Why?"

"Because Cadence did," Ivy said softly.

Hayden froze for a moment, then jerked to look at the couch where Cadence had been sitting. She was gone.

Ivy glared at Hayden. "You might not feel you've been dating long enough for marriage or have even discussed it in your relationship, but having the man you love say he refuses to marry you is going to hurt any woman."

"Crap." Hayden darted toward the front door.

"She turned left," Nelson called out behind him.

For once, Hayden didn't mind Nelson's interference. With a wave of gratitude, he ran into the night. It only took moments to find her. She had walked to the side of the house and was sitting on the ground just around the corner.

Hayden stopped in his tracks and stared down at her. Cadence refused to look up. "Hey," he said awkwardly.

"Hey," she said back.

Shoot. Now what? Slowly, in case she objected, he leaned against the house and slid down to sit on the ground with her. "So... that was kinda crazy, huh?"

Cadence pursed her lips and nodded. Her arms were resting on her knees and she was staring at her fingers.

"Look, Cadi, I'm sorry. I didn't mean it the way it sounded-"

"No, no, no. I get it, Hayden. I do." She hurried to stop him. "I mean, we've only been officially dating a few days. What would people say if we got married this quick?"

He reached over and took one of her hands, playing with her soft fingers. "I think some would say we were crazy and others would say it was romantic."

Cadence rolled her eyes and turned to look at him. "Romantic? Really?"

He shrugged and pulled her fingers closer. "You don't think it would be romantic to fall so hard and fast for someone that you couldn't wait to be with them?" He kissed one finger. "That you couldn't bear to let them go at the end of the day?" He kissed the next. "That your every thought was so consumed with them that you went against societal convention just to be with them?" He kissed another finger.

"You know, for a guy who says he's no good with the romantic stuff, you sure are handling it well right now," Cadence whispered.

Hayden smirked. "I know."

Cadence closed her eyes and gave a small laugh. "Ah, that ego never goes far, does it?"

"Maybe not, but you love me anyway."

"I know," she agreed, her voice still soft.

"Cadence, you need to know that I'm not opposed to marrying you. In fact, from the moment I knew I was in love, I knew we would get married." He continued after her jaw dropped. "Even though I did a horrible job of it, I was trying to protect *you*."

"Protect me? Hayden you stood there and flat out said you didn't want to marry me. How is that being protective?"

"Sweetheart, you have been fighting against marriage ever since you left home. I wasn't about to shove you into another one."

"Ah, but there's the difference. The first one was unwanted."

Hayden narrowed his eyes. "Are you saying you actually want to marry me?"

"Do you want to marry me?" she shot back.

"Yes." There was no hesitation in his response. "I might not have planned on it happening this early, but I told you before you were the first woman to catch my attention in years and I meant it. I'm not distracted by every pretty face that comes my way, Cadi. I'm only going to invest time in something if it's what I really want."

"And am I? What you really want?" Her eyes darted back and forth between his, hopeful, yet wary.

"More than anything," he said as he kissed her palm. "But you haven't answered the question yet, Love. What do you think about it?"

"I feel the same way." She trailed her fingers along the stubble on his chin. "I was content with Ryan, but now that I know the difference between that and what I feel now, I don't want to give it up."

Hayden stood up. "Well, then come on, Woman. We have a wedding to plan." He held out his hand and pulled her up, straight into his arms. "I told you I always get what I want," he said against her lips before kissing her.

Cadence immediately wrapped her arms around his neck and pulled him in closer.

Hayden chuckled low in his throat as he backed her up until she was against the house. For several minutes he basked in everything that was Cadence. *My Cadence. My fiancée. My soon to be wife.* The thought didn't startle him like he thought it would, instead he felt eager at the new chapter that lay ahead.

CADENCE HAD NEVER FELT so light. She was going to marry Hayden. *Oh my gosh, I'm going to marry Hayden!* Her inner girl squealed that this handsome, strong, conceited man was going to be hers. A thought hit her and she giggled, breaking their kiss.

"What?" Hayden asked, amusement in his tone.

"I was just thinking that now I never need to learn to cook. I'll have you as my personal chef," she tapped the end of his nose with her finger.

"Oh, the wishes of a princess. Hate to break it to you, Darling, but now you're going to have to learn to cook like a pro. I won't stand for anything less in my wife. I expect breakfast in bed every Sunday." Hayden grinned and pumped his eyebrows.

"How about you do the cooking and I'll do the taxes?"

"DONE!" Hayden took her hand and started to walk back to the front door. "I so got the better end of the deal."

"Not even." Cadence smiled.

"We're back," Hayden announced as they walked inside.

Cadence shivered as the warmth of the room hit her.

Hayden rubbed his hands up and down her arms. "Sorry. I shouldn't have kept you outside for so long."

"Oh, I was plenty warm while we were outside," Cadence said coyly.

"Careful, Babe. We're not married yet," Hayden said close to her ear before smacking her backside.

"Oh! Hayden!"

"So, what was decided?" Eli asked dryly as he rested on the arm of a recliner.

"Looks like we're getting married," Hayden said.

"Sweet! I'll be the only bachelor of the 'Overnight Billionaire Bachelors'! That means all the babes for me and me alone!" Nelson rubbed his hands together and cackled.

Hayden made a face and shook his head. "Seriously, I think he was dropped on his head as a baby," he said to Eli.

"I'm inclined to agree with you," Eli responded.

"Jealous! You're all just jealous!" Nelson pointed his finger at his brothers.

"Uh, no. I've got what I want." Hayden pulled Cadence in front of him and wrapped his arms around her middle.

"Pleeeease," Nelson hung his head back and closed his eyes. "No lovey-dovey stuff while I'm here. Save it for the honeymoon."

"Oh, you mean like this?" Eli bent down and began kissing Ivy, who squeaked in surprise, but quickly joined the fun.

"Or this?" Hayden began nuzzling and kissing Cadence's neck, making loud smacking noises as he went.

"Stop! I can't take it! You guys are revolting!"

Cadence giggled as Hayden continued his assault. "Hayden... stop!" she laughed.

"That's it! I'm outta here." Nelson stood and marched through the door.

Both Hayden and Eli stopped their actions and watched the door intently. When a few moments passed and nothing happened, Hayden finally spoke.

"Finally! I thought he'd never leave," he said loudly with dramatic relief in his voice.

"Now we can actually get back to business," Eli agreed.

"Just kidding!" Nelson slammed the door open and his brothers both groaned. "Despite Ivy's newfound nefariousness," he paused, "is that word?" He shook his head. "Doesn't matter. Despite that, I knew you would need my keen mind to get this all figured out."

"Do men ever grow up?" Cadence directed her question to a pink cheeked Ivy.

"Not that I can tell," Ivy responded.

"Good to know," Cadence murmured before sitting down.

Eli gave Hayden a hard look. "You better invite Laken and Teagan. They nearly shredded me when I eloped."

Hayden sighed. "Right. Let's figure out the details and we'll get them on board."

"All right. Let's plan a wedding!" Ivy squealed.

CHAPTER 18

The air in the small, bridal dressing room felt thick with nerves and anticipation. Two days ago, Cadence had said yes to Ivy's plan to marry Hayden, but now she shook with anxiety at the thought that in just a few minutes, she would become Mrs. Hayden Truman. "Are you sure about this?" Cadence asked Ivy. Her voice shook as she smoothed imaginary wrinkles in her dress.

"Absolutely. But the most important question is, are you?" Ivy stopped messing with Cadence's hair and walked around to look her in the eye. "I don't have to tell you this isn't just a pretend game." Ivy laid her hands on Cadence's shoulders. "Are you sure you want to marry Hayden? He's awfully cocky sometimes."

Cadence laughed, as intended, and the tension in the air dissipated. "Yes. Despite his arrogant attitude, I love him. I can't imagine spending my life with anyone else."

"That's what I needed to hear." Ivy's green eyes twinkled. "Now, stand up and turn around."

Cadence's knees were shaky, but she did as directed. Behind her was a mirror, and she stopped when she saw herself. Her blue eyes were bright and happiness exuded from her very countenance. The dress she wore was white, but was a cocktail style, rather than one with a long train. Her dark hair had been curled and Ivy had pinned one side up, bringing the long tresses around to hang over the opposite shoulder.

"You are so gorgeous!" Ivy said with tears in her eyes. "If you weren't going to be my sister, I'd have to hate you!"

Cadence smiled through her own tears. "Don't make me mess up my makeup!" she laughed.

"Oh, right." Ivy grabbed a tissue and handed it to Cadence.

"It feels wrong to be getting married without my parents." A small pang of sadness hit her and she took a gasping breath.

"I'm sorry they're not here," Ivy said quietly.

"Me too," Cadence responded. "But if they were, I'd be marrying a different groom."

Ivy nodded. "True enough."

Cadence took in a long breath through her nose and straightened her shoulders. "Nope. No being sad. I'm marrying the man of my dreams and I'm in Vegas. There are no tears in Vegas."

The group of siblings and spouses had managed to sneak out of their resort and fly on the Truman's private plane to Las Vegas where they were staging a "spontaneous" wedding.

Ivy walked around, eyeing Cadence's dress. "You look stunning, but boy it would have been fun to put you in one of those long, traditional dresses." Her eyes came up. "You know, like Kate Middleton wore."

"I know, but I wanted this simple. Totally opposite of what my mother would have done."

Ivy waved her off. "I know. But still." She sighed. "This is two of the Truman men that have married in a hurry. Hopefully, Nelson will give us a chance to plan something proper."

The girls looked at each other and burst out laughing.

"I don't think there's anything proper about Nelson," Cadence said as her giggling died down.

"I know," Ivy agreed.

A knock came on the door. "Can we come in?" Laken's voice carried into the room.

"Yep. We're done," Ivy responded, turning the knob.

"Oh my goodness!" Laken, the oldest of Hayden's twin sisters, put her hands to her mouth. "You look amazing! What I wouldn't give for your coloring!"

Cadence eyed Laken's shiny, dark hair and smooth, fair skin. "I don't think you have anything to worry about," Cadence said.

She had met the sisters the night before when they flew in for the wedding. Both Laken and her twin, Teagan, had recently finished their educations, and the family had been talking about them coming to work at the resort.

Cadence had been caught off guard at the difference in the two girls. They were identical in looks, but definitely not personality.

"You look beautiful," Teagan's quiet voice said from behind Laken.

"Thank you, Teagan." Cadence smiled warmly. Teagan's studious manner meant she was often in the back and easily overlooked, but Cadence found her company to be very pleasant when she spoke.

"All right. Does everyone remember the plan? You girls have to watch from far enough back that you don't get caught on camera. If people see you, they won't believe that this is truly a last minute wedding." Ivy looked around at everyone.

Laken rolled her eyes. "Got it." She folded her arms and huffed. "At least this time we're invited. Unlike when Eli ran down the aisle."

Cadence watched Ivy's cheeks begin to turn red, but the girl stood her ground. "I'm sure Hayden is happy to have you. Now, let's go."

The girls filed out of the small dressing room and headed toward the foyer of the chapel they were in.

"Chapel of Love," Cadence snorted. "Could we have picked anything more cliche?"

"I know, right?" Ivy laughed. "But it fits with the story we're selling, so..." She shrugged.

Once they were at the doors of the chapel, Ivy started giving out directions. "Laken, Teagan, you two go on in and stand off to the side. Cadence, give me two minutes to set up in the wings before you come through the door, all right? I'm going to try and make it look like an employee is secretly taping your wedding. That way when we 'leak,'" she used her fingers for quotation marks, "it to the press, no one will question anything."

"Yeah, yeah. We've been over all this." Laken flipped her hair over her shoulder and threw open the door. "Come on, Teags. Let's go."

Teagan smiled at Cadence and Ivy. "Thank you for including us. I'm thrilled to be gaining another sister." She squeezed Cadence's hand and slipped through the doorway.

"I would be too, if Laken was my sister," Ivy said under her breath.

Cadence's eyes shot open, and she bit her lips to keep from laughing.

Ivy slapped her hand over her mouth. "Shoot. Someday I really need to get a filter. Geez, Louise." Shaking her head, she grinned ruefully at Cadence. "Showtime!" With a pump of her eyebrows, she handed Cadence a small bouquet of long-stemmed roses and disappeared through the door.

A mass of butterflies burst to life in Cadence's stomach. "I can't believe I'm actually doing this," she murmured. Her breathing picked up, and she grew overly warm. She paced back and forth in front of the chapel doors, her stilettos clicking against the tile floor and fanned herself. "You love him, Cadence. Everything will be alright. You love him."

Taking a deep breath, she straightened her dress and her shoulders and put her hand on the door. "Here we go."

With a determined push, she opened the door and began to walk down the aisle.

Music played in the background, but Cadence didn't notice it or the family members hidden throughout the room. One hand strangled the flowers to death, and the other pressed against those darn butterflies. *Holy cow...*

Hayden stood in a white shirt and black pants. No tie hung around his neck, but Cadence didn't think he needed one. His semi-casual vibe was absolutely perfect. His dark eyes connected with hers and suddenly, the world righted itself. It didn't matter that they had rushed into this wedding, nothing had ever felt so right.

Hayden smiled enticingly and rather than wait for her to come to him, he started taking steps in her direction. With a too-wide smile of her own, Cadence pushed her feet into action.

Between the two of them, they covered the ground quickly. Hayden's hand found the back of her neck and he pulled her in for a thorough kiss.

It wasn't until a throat cleared that they were brought back to the real world.

Hayden rested his forehead against hers while he caught his breath. "There are no words to describe how you look tonight."

Cadence's already flushed cheeks grew even hotter. "You don't look so bad yourself," she said breathlessly.

"You ready for this?"

Smiling, Cadence nodded.

Stepping back, Hayden offered his arm and led her up to where the officiator waited.

FIFTEEN MINUTES. ALL it took was fifteen minutes for my life to change forever. Hayden watched as his wife hugged his family and received congratulations from them.

Ivy had stopped filming and everyone had come to the center of the room for the small reception.

"Congrats, little brother," Eli said with a shoulder slap.

Hayden nodded. He was still in shock from the events, but at the same time, knew it was the best decision he had ever made.

"I wasn't sure we'd ever see the day a woman tamed the great Chef Truman," Nelson snickered.

"I'll show you tamed," Hayden said with a grin. He swiped an arm at Nelson, who ducked away playfully.

"Boys, now is not the time," Laken scolded, tossing her hair over her shoulder.

Teagan walked up to Hayden and hugged his arm. "Congratulations, Hay. I like her a lot."

Hayden gave a crooked grin. This quiet, little beauty held a special place in his heart. Although their personalities seemed to be polar opposites, Teagan and Hayden had always gotten along well. Both of them knew what it was to be ostracized but Teagan didn't have Hayden's fire for fighting back. He had protected her since they were kids and even now, he checked in with her often. *Unlike me and Laken. She's so spoiled, she drives me crazy.* "Thanks, Teags," he said, patting her arm. "I like her a lot too."

"Well, I should hope so!" she teased with a smile. "In fact, I hope you like her enough to save her from Laken."

Hayden's eyes shot toward his wife. *Wife. This is so nuts.* He saw that Teagan was right as usual. Laken was going on about something and Cadence's face clearly showed she wanted out.

"Go quick, or Laken will convince her to dye her hair blonde or something," Teagan said with a push.

"Not on my watch," Hayden growled and pushed his way to Cadence's side. He immediately grabbed Cadence around the waist and planted a kiss on the side of her head.

"Hay! I wasn't done with her yet," Laken whined.

"Anything you have to say can wait. My wife and I have a very important appointment." He felt Cadence's body relax in his arms.

"Right. Thanks for the advice, Laken." She turned to Hayden. "Are we ready to go?"

"Whenever you are," he said softly.

A slow smile crept across Cadence's face. "Then let's get a move on."

"Okey doke, folks. I'm uploading the video to a couple of news stations now and I've sent a warning text to Ryan so he's got his game face on when everything breaks." Ivy looked up from her phone with a solemn expression. "Good luck with your parents. I'm sure that's not going to be the most pleasant conversation."

Hayden gave Cadence a squeeze to let her know he was there, but the sheen of tears was evident in her eyes and he knew it wasn't going to be a breezy honeymoon.

"Thanks everyone. We'll see you in a couple weeks." Hayden pointed a finger at Eli. "You better keep track of my kitchen. If someone messes things up, I'm gonna-"

"Not today, Hayden!" Cadence cut off his threat and pulled him toward the door. "James and Eli are plenty capable of running things while you're gone. Now, come on."

"Yes, Chef. Thank you, Chef," he said with a grin.

"And don't you forget it," Cadence retorted.

The two of them headed out the front doors toward a waiting limo while the rest of the family slipped out the back to avoid being seen.

"Whew. That wasn't as bad as I thought," Cadence said as they slid inside the vehicle waiting to take them to the airport.

"The story hasn't hit yet, that's why. Give it ten minutes and all heck will break loose."

"I know." Her blue eyes caught Hayden's. "I can't believe we're married."

Hayden waggled his eyebrows. "Believe it, Cupcake. You're mine now."

Cadence leaned in and kissed his jaw. "No complaints here."

"Better not be," Hayden murmured as he turned his head and took her lips.

Cadence's phone buzzed, breaking up their first real kiss as man and wife. Glancing down, she stiffened. "It's them."

"Already? Geez, that was quick." Hayden scrubbed his hands down his face. "You ready?"

"Nope. But I don't think that matters." Cadence answered the call. "Hey, Dad."

"Our publicist just picked up a rumor online that can't be true," Noah Everwood started without so much as a 'hello'.

"Oh? And what is that?"

"Someone claims to have seen you leaving a Las Vegas wedding chapel with that chef guy. But I know my Cadi-Bear wouldn't do something like that."

Cadence gripped Hayden's hand and his heart ached. *What do I do? How do I help take this burden from her? She's mine to protect and right now I'm useless.*

"Well," Cadence cleared her throat, "someone must be awfully speedy on social media, because it is true."

"WHAT?" A loud, feminine screech came across the line and there was an obvious scuffle on the other side of the line. Her mother's voice came screaming through the speaker. "You disrespectful brat! How could you do something like that? After all the work we've done! All the money we've spent! What is Ryan going to say? He'll be heartbroken! We had everything ready for next month and you've ruined it!"

Hayden grabbed the phone out of Cadence's hand where it dangled precariously. Tears poured down her cheeks, and she was doing her best to wipe them away.

"Mrs. Everwood, if you would just calm down for a minute," Hayden said loudly into the cell.

"Who is this? Are you the man she married?"

"Yes. This is Hayden Truman, Cadi's husband. Now you need to understand-"

"What did you do to my daughter? Ever since she's worked for you and your brothers, she's become a completely different person. I won't stand for this." Her voice backed away from the phone. "Noah. Send a car. We're bringing her home now instead of next week."

"Mrs. Everwood, Cadi and I are headed on our honeymoon. If you would like to see her, you're going to have to wait until we get back," Hayden said through clenched teeth. *It's a miracle that Cadence turned out to be who she is with this shrew living with her all those years.*

"Now, you listen to me," Arianna's voice had dropped to a deadly calm. "If you go on that honeymoon, I am through. I will disown her so fast it will make your head swim. Her inheritance will be gone and she will never be welcome in my house again."

Shouting could be heard in the background but Hayden couldn't tell what was being said. He glanced at Cadence's miserable face and raised a questioning eyebrow. "Your call," he mouthed. Pride like he'd never known soared through every inch of him when she hugged his arm and leaned her head on his shoulder.

"Well, then I guess this is hello and goodbye, Mrs. Everwood. I don't think it's too big of a loss though." Before the screeching could get any louder, he hung up the phone and turned it off.

"Guess we didn't even need the video after all. It's just gonna be fuel for the fire. It's done. And we're done. No technology for us for the next two weeks, okay?" He leaned down so he could see her face.

"Sounds good to me," Cadence said with a sigh. Her eyes were closed and a look of contentment was on her face. "I should feel terrible, but for some reason, I feel as if a huge burden has been lifted off me. I was so blind and then so angry. She and my dad have used me as a commodity for so long, but now I'm actually free. I wish it hadn't meant I had to cut ties with them, but I can't be sorry the fight is finally over."

"Oh, I'm not sure your mother is going to give up quite so easily. But still, there's nothing they can do to hurt us now. You're mine and once we actually get to Fiji," he put a finger under her chin and lifted her face, "I'll have all the time in the world to show you just how much," he kissed her cheeks, "I love you." He continued to rain kisses around her face until finally working his way to her lips.

"It sounds like paradise," Cadence sighed. "Thank you, Hayden. Thank you for everything. You're the reason this is all worth it."

Hayden grinned. "I know," he quipped, then cut off Cadence's laugh with more serious matters.

EPILOGUE
6 months later

Strong arms slipped around Cadence from behind and a scruffy chin rested where her shoulder and neck met.

"Good morning, Handsome," she said to Hayden as he yawned.

"Morning, Beautiful. Whatcha doing?"

"Making my first batch of non-burned pancakes."

Hayden eyed the stack of dark, but not black, flapjacks sitting next to the stovetop. "Are you sure about that? I think they're supposed to be- Oof!" He grunted when Cadence elbowed him in the stomach.

"Lay off! These are my best ones yet!"

"Of course they are," he soothed as his arms went back around her. "I'm proud of you."

"As you should be," Cadence said cheekily.

"I'll grab the plates and syrup." Hayden let go of her and walked to the cupboard. "You never did tell me what you chatted with your dad about last night."

The familiar ache that accompanied thoughts of her family had dulled slightly as the months wore on, but Cadence was sure it would never completely go away. "Nothing new. It was just one of his normal check ins, but Mom still won't acknowledge she has a daughter."

"Sorry, Sweetheart," Hayden kissed her cheek. "Give her time, she might still come around." He turned back to setting the table. "I saw on the news that Ryan has a new girlfriend."

Cadence laughed. "He's been completely enjoying his time in the limelight. He's been seen with some Hollywood Starlet. Rumors vary as to how serious they are."

"Good for him, I guess. Can't say it appeals to me."

"I don't know, you seemed pretty happy with your media blitz last month when you got your Michelin stars." Cadence brought the plate of pancakes to the table and sat down.

Hayden grinned and flexed his muscles. "I've told you, I always get what I want."

Cadence rolled her eyes. After saying a quick blessing, they dug into the food.

"So, I was thinking..." Cadence glanced sideways at her husband.

"Hmm?" Hayden kept chewing but looked up at her.

"I've been thinking I should become a baker."

Hayden's face fell. "What? Why would you want to do that?"

Cadence bit the inside of her lip to keep from laughing. "Well, don't you think I'd be good at it?"

His face turned red and Hayden rubbed the back of his neck. "Sweetheart, I thought we agreed you'd do the taxes, and I'd do the cooking. Don't you think we should stick to that arrangement?"

"Nope." Cadence took a bite. "I mean, it's already too late, anyway."

Hayden scowled. "What are you talking about? What's too late?"

"It's too late for me to not be a baker."

Hayden scrubbed his hands down his face. "I'm so lost."

"Well, I've managed to already put a bun in the oven, so..." Cadence kept eating while she watched the emotions flit over Hayden's face.

"Are you serious?"

She smiled.

Hayden laughed and stood from his seat. Reaching out his hand, he pulled her up for a sweet kiss then tucked her under his chin. "I hope she has your blue eyes," he said against the top of her head.

"And if it's a boy?"

"Nope. No boys. I'm too afraid he'll end up like Nelson."

Cadence laughed and leaned in for another kiss. "You're terrible."

"And yet you love me."

"Always and forever."

I just adore fun banter between couples,

don't you? And I have to admit that
I find cooking together sooo romantic,
so I LOVED being able to play with that
In this story. :)
If you're not quite ready to be done
With the romance, never fear!
Nelson's story is up next in
"Her Fake Billionaire Boyfriend"

Other Books by Laura Ann

**All stories are sweet, clean romances with a guaranteed Happy
Ever After,
FREE in KU**

The Overnight Billionaire Bachelor Series
What happens when three brothers find a hidden treasure?
Paparazzi, drama and troubles on the path to true love, that's what!
Her Billionaire Boss[1]
Her Billionaire Chef[2]
Her Fake Billionaire Boyfriend[3]
Her Billionaire Gardener[4]
The Billionaire's Best Friend[5]

It's All About the Mistletoe Series
How do six friends decide to stand up to a bully at the Christmas Ball?
By bringing fake boyfriends, of course!
Too bad they didn't take the power of a certain Christmas tradition in-
to account.
Mistletoe Magic[6]

---

1. https://www.amazon.com/dp/B07P8X4HY1

2. https://www.amazon.com/dp/B07NSPM976

3. https://www.amazon.com/dp/B07RL4PRTM

4. https://www.amazon.com/dp/B07T1DS622

5. https://www.amazon.com/dp/B07VNHCXKZ

<u>Mistletoe Mayhem</u>[7]
<u>Mister Mistletoe</u>[8]
<u>Mistletoe Mistake</u>[9]
<u>Mistletoe Memories</u>[10]
<u>Mistletoe Maverick</u>[11]

---

6. https://www.amazon.com/dp/B07YN723B6

7. https://www.amazon.com/dp/B07YN7LR2F

8. https://www.amazon.com/dp/B07YM426PJ

9. https://www.amazon.com/dp/B07YN726CL

10. https://www.amazon.com/dp/B07YN8BQYM

11. https://www.amazon.com/dp/B07YN8G3CJ

<u>Middleton Prep Series</u>
Contemporary Romance with a Fairy Tale Twist!
<u>A Home for the Ugly Duckling</u>[12]
<u>The Librarian and Her Beast</u>[13]
<u>Ms. Cinder's Prince</u>[14]
<u>Waking Ms. Briar</u>[15]
<u>A Date for the Goose Girl</u>[16]
<u>Running from the Wolf</u>[17]
<u>Ms. Frogg's Hidden Billionaire</u>[18]
<u>Saving Ms. Gothel</u>[19]
<u>A Billionaire for Ms. Snow</u>[20]
<u>Goldilock's Misunderstood Billionaire</u>[21]

---

12. https://www.amazon.com/dp/B07FKYQ3QB

13. https://www.amazon.com/dp/B07D1BC8CF

14. https://www.amazon.com/dp/B07D9VMPW8

15. https://www.amazon.com/dp/B07F47NZMF

16. https://www.amazon.com/dp/B07G4GDRCD

17. https://www.amazon.com/dp/B07H51DK9G

18. https://www.amazon.com/dp/B07HZ5YD34

19. https://www.amazon.com/dp/B07K36DTMC

20. https://www.amazon.com/dp/B07MF36J2Y

21. https://www.amazon.com/dp/B07N818YYG